Murder Without Tears

MURDER
WITHOUT TEARS

LEONARD LUPTON

WILDSIDE PRESS

MURDER WITHOUT TEARS

1

I KEPT watching the door. Yesterday she had come through that door. I had the feeling that she would come through that door again today in spite of the heat.

It was cool in the barroom. These old Hudson River houses, built by the brickyard owners, had a depth and dimension that offset humidity and June sunlight. I sat there in the caned chair at the round table with the checkered cloth and wondered what old Jason Prescott would have thought of my turning his mansion into a fashionable ginmill. I wondered what my old man would have thought of it, also. He had been straw boss at the Prescott brickyard. He had given them a service, a loyalty, a real humility that has gone out of date today. And a good thing it has.

I got a lot of satisfaction out of seeing the Prescott mansion turned into a roadhouse.

Of course it isn't any waterfront dive. It's five miles north of Newburyport on the Hudson River; up where the big estates still keep two or three gardeners each to tend the rolling, shaded lawns that always were and still are Off Limits to the likes of us Broomes.

Broome. When I was a kid I used to ask myself how anyone with a name like that could get to be President. My old man used to have a wry way of looking at life

7

and he didn't take my complaint very seriously. "Sure you could be President some day," he used to tell me. "Think of the campaign slogan—'Let a new Broome sweep clean!'"

He never took himself or his family name or his position in life very seriously. I don't suppose he ever looked up from the job in the brickyard and wondered what it would be like to live in the big, square, brick house on the hill.

But I did. And now I knew. It took a war and a government loan and a muddle-witted ex-bootlegger to make it possible. But here I was, sitting in the big house. And that wasn't all.

I was waiting and watching for a woman to come through that door again. To see me. One of the women who belonged up here on the hill.

I could hear pans and kettles clattering in the kitchen. I pay my chef one-fifty and keep, and the pastry chef almost as much. That's good money up here. In the summer, for the lunch hour, my waiters wear white; but for the dinner hour they dress the part. I've tried to serve the best *filet mignon* in this part of the Valley and I've done something else—I've reversed the usual trend. I've tried to make my place hard to get into. It works.

Of course downstairs in the barroom it's different. The barroom is a replica of the saloon my old man used to go to down on the flats. Everybody invited, though mostly only the right people come.

There are brass spittoons, and sawdust on the floor, and a white marble rail in front of the mahogany at just the right height to balance a tray of beer. There are mirrors all around the walls and one day a magazine illustrator, up here in the valley to release his blood pressure over a week-end, piled the rye too high on the rocks and paid off by soaping the mirrors with the kind of art that fits in

8

well with the phony kerosene lights that have been set up
in wall brackets all around the place.

The place looks like it used to look when it was down
on the flats, except that the sheriff and the ambulance
never come out here on a Saturday night; for the trade
I get even here is the silk lapel trade and there are as
many feminine shoulders, bare to cleavage as the British
say, as there are dinner jackets.

It's quite a way of life and most of the time I'm feeling
a little smug and satisfied about it. My accountant says
I'm making money and I'm having a subtle kind of revenge
on the Prescott memory, just to pay them back for what
they did to my old man. But every now and again I could
still get the feeling that something was wrong.

You grow up like I did, all full of steam and ambition,
and spend thirty years trying to climb maybe three or
four hundred feet up a hill, and when you get there maybe
you too would find that the view was wonderful and the
air different—but the people merely the way you'd figured
they would be.

I thought about all this while I kept watching the door.
I don't often worry about myself, or waste time looking
in mirrors. But now I took a look at the wall mirror and
worried a little. What would she see when she came in?
I'm not tall like a knight on a white charger. My shoulders
are too heavy and my jaw is too broad—and now I was
fretting about the mustache that I had grown in the army
to make me look older. It was no hair-line thing, but one
of these Robert Preston type mustaches. I had wondered if
I'd better shave it off. But that seemed a silly thing to do,
now. She had seemed to like me with the mustache—after
all, she was coming back.

I sat there and thought about her. It had happened last
night. She had come in with another girl. They had both
been in evening dress. She was just back from the Coast.

I hadn't found out yet what she'd been doing out there. I didn't think it could have been the studios. She didn't seem that type. Pretty enough? Sure—well, maybe not exactly pretty. What do you mean by pretty?

The feeling I got from her was not of prettiness, but of impact. Something hit me. For the first time since the war something hit me where it matters.

I remember what I thought. I thought, *there's a good-sized doll* . . . and let it go at that for a minute. It shook me up a little, later, to realize that if I'd employed a floorman or a bouncer I might never have got to talk to her.

They had taken a table, just the two of them. They didn't seem to notice that they were the only unescorted women in the place. I stopped at the table and they looked up from whatever they'd been saying. I've seen the time when it might have thrown me to come face to face with so much poise and assurance. But I'd picked up a little poise along the way, too. I think maybe the army helped. That's no wisecrack. I mean it. Going through O.C.S., even infantry, and getting the gold bar—I know. There's a gag about it. Gentleman, by act of congress.

Skip the gag. I thought I was going to lead a platoon into battle. I could field-strip an MI, a carbine, a .30 water-cooled, and a .50 air-cooled and jumble them together blindfolded and then reassemble the parts. That was considered pretty damned important. I knew how to level a mortar baseplate, make out a morning report, and what to do until the medic got there. Maybe even more important, I knew the first thing the medic would do when he did get there. Oh, I was a well-instructed 2nd Lt. of Inf.

So I became a maintenance officer in the headquarters company of a supply battalion in an armored division—me, who didn't know a spanner wrench from a socket. A maintenance officer and, automatically, a gentleman.

Maybe it should have happened to somebody else. Maybe

MURDER WITHOUT TEARS

I would have been better off if I had never found out about being a gentleman. It caused me some misery along the way because some of the men I had to deal with were gentlemen, and not by any act of congress. But I had the great advantage of being treated like a gentleman and after a while I began to act like a gentleman, and sometimes even to think like one. And so I stood at the round table and looked down at these two girls, all of whose male ancestors had been gentlemen for generations back, and I was neither embarrassed nor distressed.

I didn't want to make any particular fuss about it, but I wanted them to understand clearly and at once just what sort of a position they had put me in. I smiled and said, "If I may?" and sat down before they said I couldn't. I said, "We're always most happy to welcome new guests, and since it's the first rule of the house that there shall be no unescorted ladies present, I'm going to take advantage of the situation and pretend that I'm escorting both of you tonight. Fair enough?"

I remember that the brunette smiled, but for the first time in my life I didn't pay much attention to a brunette. I was looking at the blonde. She was neither a bright and glittering blonde nor a grubby imitation one. She was a girl with fluffy, curly, very attractive gold-colored hair. I mean that literally. If you're not too young, you've got a token gold piece around the house somewhere and remembering it, you will know at once the color of Anne Cramer's hair.

She told me her name almost at once. I suspect that she wanted to impress me at the very start—make sure that I wouldn't for a minute misconstrue her purpose in being here. Everyone in the township knew the name of Cramer. It might ring a bell with you, too, if you heard the full title that her father wore with distinction. Brigadier-General Gunther Cramer.

To a former second lieutenant of infantry it was pretty impressive.

I got my breath back and said, "I'll bet you played in this house as a kid. I mean—the Prescotts and the Cramers and the—" for a minute I couldn't think of any of the other old and impressive family names. In my boyhood there had been room only for a villain and a hero. Prescott had been the villain, but time and the clay pits had taken care of him. Now here was the hero's daughter.

She laughed and said, "Yes," and gave me an odd, straightforward look. "I played here as a child with Sue Prescott and when I came home yesterday and heard that the old mansion was now a—"

"Ginmill?" I said softly.

"Exactly," she said in her soft, grave voice. She looked at me very steadily and I thought that she was going to ask me how I could have done such a thing, as though it were some kind of desecration. But she didn't ask anything. She sat looking at me as though an explanation from me would be her natural right.

I didn't hurry to answer. I saw her jaw was broad and firm. Her skin was very good, creamy and tight-textured. Her clear, appraising eyes hinted at a secret boldness. I thought the traditional thing—spoiled, rich brat. But then I knew that I was using the worn-out thoughts of other people, not my own, and tried to reassess her and fit a new thought to that face.

Before I could get anywhere with the idea she was after me with words.

"How did you happen to do this?" she said. "This isn't a cocktail lounge, this is a replica of the old barroom down on the flats. I remember my father telling about it. It was a grim and terrible place."

I looked around the room. I inhaled my cigar slowly and came back to her. "It isn't grim or terrible here, is it?

12

The same bar, the same fixtures, the same sort of tables and caned chairs. Even the kerosene lamps along the wall came from down on the flats. But the sheriff has never been here, the ambulance has never backed up outside that door. It must be true that God made two kinds of people —the rich are better-mannered. When we get the others, they behave."

There was amusement away back in her eyes.

"When I heard that a man named Jason Broome was running River House, I tried to place the name. The last name. I could understand about the Jason. For generations, the oldest male Prescott was always named Jason. That suggested that your father might have worked for Jason Prescott."

"He was a straw boss in the brickyards when I was a kid. He died the week after the yards closed down."

"And in your mind," she said, "that took on some twisted significance. You blamed Jason Prescott for your father's death. And turning the Prescott mansion into a roadhouse was your idea of a subtle revenge."

I could look at her and not mind. I could laugh at her. I had her then, caught and trapped by her own words.

I said, "Prescott didn't close the yards down for the sake of a whim. He ran out of clay. No clay, no brick. And my father died of pneumonia, caught duck-hunting out of season. It had nothing to do with a broken heart and the loss of a job after a lifetime given to it, if that's what you mean."

"Then why this hatred? Why this flaunting in the face? Why bring a fine old house and fine old memories to such an end?"

I let the laughter in me show, and if she wished to read the mockery also, why, that was there too.

"An ex-bootlegger by name of Gallagher bought the place at a tax sale, fixed it up and got a license. I was in the army at the time and the last thought I had in mind was running a roadhouse in the Hudson Valley. Now, may I bring you something from the bar?"

She said, "Scotch and soda. Eloise, too." I remembered that she had not presented me to the brunette. She thought of it at the same time and said, "I'm sorry. I was too taken up with history. Eloise, this is Jason Broome, our host. Eloise Ruysdale, Mr. Broome."

I said, "How do you do?" I thought that if I had any sense I would pay some attention to Eloise Ruysdale. She was a brunette and I had always liked the dark ones. But I found it difficult in the presence of Anne Cramer—only she came through at the moment.

I came back from the bar with the three glasses. I know that it is poor practice to drink with the customer—I haven't the paunch for it and I don't really like the stuff. But I knew an occasion, and this was one.

Anne Cramer said, "It was nice of you not to have us thrown out. I've only just come in from the Coast. They aren't so particular in some of the cocktail lounges out there."

I smiled and said, "There are places along the side streets down in Newburyport where they aren't so particular, either. Every so often someone writes a piece about it for a newspaper or magazine and a license gets revoked. I try to be a practical businessman."

"You seem to have been very practical, Mr. Broome. But I have the feeling that Eloise and I are keeping you from your work." Anne Cramer stood up and, of course, I stood up too. I had a really good look at her then, full length. She was as tall as I—it was difficult to tell much else about her except that she was not obviously misshapen. There are so many ways to improve on nature today that a man is a fool to take all he sees as evidence of perfection.

But she was wearing a summer evening gown and a

summer fur and the rest seemed to be all her own. I liked what I saw and was trying to think how I could prolong this meeting or at least get some assurance that there would be another, when she spoke.

She said, "It has been an interesting evening—I'm really sorry about an engagement made earlier. I'd like to know more about how you have changed the Prescott mansion into River House."

I said, "Tomorrow?"

She said, "Tomorrow, then."

There was a considerable crowd in the room. We worked our way to the door. I was wondering whether to go as far as her car with them, across the blue gravel. But she gave me her hand, briefly, and with no hidden pressure that I could detect.

There had to be the rest of the evening, but I moved through it without conscious reflexes. There were suddenly things that needed thinking about.

It is easy, now, with hindsight, to know what I should have done. But at the moment no one on earth could have persuaded me to go down and jump in the river and not hold my breath. No one told me about the clay pit, for of course no one had thought of the clay pit in years. And even if they had, they would not have associated it with me or with Anne Cramer.

Or with murder.

2

I KEPT watching the door. Yesterday she had come through that door. I had the feeling that she would come through that door again today in spite of the heat.

It was still morning, too early for trade.

Everywhere, except at the round table where I sat, the caned chairs were legs-up on the other tables in the barroom. The sawdust, which was an important part of the decor, had been swept up and the floors of the front room and the back room and the office were being mopped. They are water-mopped every day, for that's the way it used to be down on the flats where the original of this room had its being.

The Prescott mansion, now known as River House, sits only a hundred feet back from the highway. There is a blue gravel drive and a blue gravel parking space near where Jason Prescott had an iron hitching post. The hitching post is now in the cellar of the carriage house and I must remember to have it set up some time. There is a whole new generation coming up that never saw a hitching post.

Finally I walked down the drive and wouldn't admit to myself that I was walking toward the road to see if her car was coming. It was a green Mercury, I remembered from last night, and there was no reason it should be coming out the River Road at this hour of the morning. But it was.

I leaned against a brick gatepost higher than my head and when the car stopped I was on the driver's side. I leaned on the window, looked in and said, "It's an early thirst you have, ma'm."

She said, "Come now, didn't you invite me for breakfast?"

A part of my mind was thinking, *She's not the innocent child she seems* . . . The other part was thinking, *Sacred Cow—this is the daughter of General Gunther Cramer—and my old man was a brickyard straw boss* . . . And just as suddenly I knew that whatever I was thinking was wholly unimportant. What mattered was what she was thinking.

She slid across the seat and said, "Do you want to go for a drive or do you want to park it for me?"

I got under the wheel and hesitated. "You spoke about breakfast—" I said tentatively.

"Conversation piece. I breakfasted hours ago. I've been out in the gardens. I might settle for lunch."

"Then it's a drive you want," I said.

"Not much of a drive. Just down on the flats. With someone who knows his way around—who remembers."

I said, "There's nothing down under the hill now. The brickyards are gone. The clay is gone from the pits. The stores are boarded up and the houses mostly fallen in on themselves."

"A ghost town," she said. She reached over and put her hand on my arm and said, "Broome—I'd ilke to see the place that spawned you. One day I'll tell you why."

I said, "Then it's not just my charm or my masculine appeal?"

"You've got it, after a fashion," she said. "It's not very overwhelming yet. But this hasn't anything to do with that.

17

Once when I was in Naples I went to see Pompeii—and if the comparison isn't too ridiculous, I'm prepared to approach your brickyard ghost town in the same mood."

I backed the smooth, green Mercury out of my blue-graveled drive, swung the wheel over and started down the hill toward the flat country along the river's edge. I said, "I don't see anything ridiculous about the comparison. People lived and loved and died in both places—and in both places a fault in nature brought the end of an era. They died a little quicker in Pompeii—none of them starved to death. That's the chief difference."

I had the feeling that she was looking at me closely, studying me, but when I took time for a glance, her hands were in her lap and she was looking straight ahead, down the hill.

I turned back to the business of driving. Halfway down the hill was the old brick school which I had entered with dread each fall and fled from in joy each June. The windows were gone now and some genius had managed to get a rock the size of my head up on the slate roof. It had cracked the slates, but hadn't gone through.

"You went to school there," she said. It was not a question.

I slowed. "Why not? Would you care to see the bronze plaque that marks the site of my old desk?"

She touched my arm again. "Bitter?" she said. "Why?"

"Not bitter, no. Just making like Berle. Why don't you laugh it up?"

"Why don't you get funny?" she said.

I drove on past the standing chimney and the weed-filled depression that marked the beginning of the old yards. Narrow-gauge track, rusted to the color of weak cocoa, still lay on rotted ties across the flats. Nature had been busy here with its chlorophyl cure-all, neatly growing

18

the green stuff over the desolation. You could hardly mark the presence of a dead community.

She said, "Is that a barge, down in there by the stream?"

I said, "It's a half-sunken brick scow on the mud bottom of the canal."

"There's a dirt road that seems to go down that way."

"You're sure you want ot go that way? There's nothing down in there but the old clay pits."

"I've never seen those," she said.

"Just holes in the ground. Some with enough pitch and drainage to keep them caked dry in midsummer—others are ponds now, with nothing to tell you that, fifty feet down, men and mules worked hard under the summer sun."

We bumped down a dim trail that was no longer a road. Cicadas droned and once we saw a blacksnake slither off through the weeds. The hill was always above us, behind us now; but at one place a dip in the trail made it seem that the river, the bank of the river, was above us, too, in the other direction. An oil tanker, southbound, rode high against the tide, a slather of white wake creaming to yellow froth at its propeller thrash.

"Look," she said, excited at the discovery, "why doesn't the river flow in here and flood this place?"

"It's the sun's heat on the flats that makes us seem lower than the river—actually this strip never floods. The houses used to be here, and the sheds over there."

There was broken brick and brick dust everywhere—the rubble of an industry that had sprung up and thrived and created a fortune and collapsed again because of the lack of the clay upon which it had been built.

She said, "And you lived here? Along this row, somewhere?"

"The biggest ruins—over there a little apart from the other ruins. My old man was Prescott's straw boss. There

19

were two foremen, but my old man used to boss the actual making of the brick."

"Brick," she said. "Somehow you never think of lives being dedicated to it. How is it made?"

I said, "There is a difference of opinion there, even in the yards. I can tell you the mixture in the old Prescott yards, but not the exact proportions—not even today."

"What went into it?"

"Sand, coal dust and clay. Does that answer your question?"

She said, "No. I think I'd like to know more about the making of brick. I'd like to picture these yards active again, and the people here as they were in the old days."

I knew what she meant. Her enthusiasm didn't make much sense, but I could understand it. The ghost towns of the West have their fans. There are clubs concerned with the preservation of old automobiles. Somewhere in New England there is a museum devoted to the bygone steamboat days. So why shouldn't she be interested in the artifacts of a vanished brickyard?

It was impossible to go farther along the rutted trail by car. I cut the switch and she said, "Can't we get out and go on foot? I'd like to see that old scow close up."

We could see the tilted cabin of the old brick barge—the rotting hulk was canted over like a drunken dowager, her broad bottom flat to the mud.

"Why not?" I said and got out. When I rounded the car, she was already waiting for me. The underbrush grew close on either side of the car and when I came abreast of her, our shoulders touched. I had seen her shoulders bare the night before, but this actual touch showed me for the first time how firmly fleshed she was.

I had been aware from the first that in many ways Anne Cramer was unlike any of the other women I had known.

It was too soon to say what special quality she possessed, but I had the feeling, even then, that it was not a quality of goodness. There was a half shadow on the earth, although the Valley in June is famous for the brightness of its summer sun. It would take a thin-veined poet to hint that the warm stillness of the flats was burdened with more than humidity, that it was a foreboding that weighted down the morning air. And since I am pleased to be neither thin-veined nor a poet, I could be amused at the idea. But not quite at peace with the world—the beginning, then, of never again being quite at peace with the world, forever after. Spare the Amen.

I stood on the bank of the inlet, which was part inlet and part man-made canal, and said, "There is your brick barge, your romantic scow. On such as this, with canopy yet, Cleopatra floated down the Nile. On such as this a million, a billion, perhaps even a trillion brick floated down the Hudson—to build Brooklyn."

She stood there on the grassy bank and was silent for a moment or two. I wondered for the first time if she were just a degree or two removed, one way or the other, from normal.

Finally she said, "A man and a woman probably lived together in that shack on that scow, once upon a time. The lazy, cat-heat of the sun would be in their bones all day, and the whisper of the night breeze would lave over them like tropic waters, soothing, cooling, reviving—"

I wanted to jolt her out of it. I lied. I said, "I remember that very scow, as a kid. The captain was a scurvy old rumpot with pellagra, and the slattern in dirty calico who cooked for him weighed over two hundred pounds and had a harelip."

She hit me with the back of her palm, not viciously, not enough to hurt. But in the nature of a warning.

21

"I can dream, can't I?" she said lightly. But I had caught the wrist of the hand that had struck me and now I shifted my grip to the upper arm and then to the shoulder. She turned to me, her face coming closer and closer as though from a great distance, far beyond my reach. And then suddenly there was no distance left between us at all and she was not beyond my reach, and the experience of vital contact that had come from the mere brushing of our shoulders was a hundredfold increased . . .

I kissed her.

She was shaking a little when she moved away, and I do not think that her eyes quite focused, for she stood for a moment with her hands on my shoulders and her face turned earthward. Her voice seemed incredibly far away when she spoke, and not her natural voice at all.

She said, "Never do that again, Jason. Never."

And I was so surprised at my own reaction to those unbelievable thirty seconds that I said, "No, Anne. Not if that's the way you want it—" but I lied, in words and tone, and she guessed at the lie and looked up at me. Suddenly she laughed, and for the moment everything was all right again—almost.

"You were telling me about the clay pit," she said. "Before we leave I should like to see it." She turned her back on the old barge which had so interested her only a few minutes before.

I said, "We'll have to go around to the other side of the yards to see the clay pit. There are a half dozen small depressions where they probed for clay, but the big pit, the pit that kept the yards going for so many years, is off here to the south."

We reached the car and I had to back it out to the road. When we reached the ruins of the old settlement near the sheds I swung the wheel over and found the rutted trail to the clay pit. I stopped at the shore of a barren, water-filled depression. The top branches of a crabapple tree were just above water level at the end of the lake nearest us, and we could see where the morning sun slanted down through ash-gray spidery branches, waterlogged now and barren of blossoms these many years past.

"This is it?" she asked. "This lake is a clay pit?"

"Yes," I said.

I glanced at the sun and was sure that it was about right for us to see what I wanted her to see. I led her to the edge of the pond and said, "Look down at an angle, just about in a line with that sumac tree over there." I waited, and she made a sound of surprise.

"What is it?" she said. "A wagon of some kind—and just where the sun strikes I can see a sloping shelf and the roof of a building." She shivered. "Is there a world down there still, going on about its business under water?"

I laughed, not yet understanding the unusual trend that her thoughts could take. I said, "That's an old shed where they kept tools. The sloping shelf is the road out. And the strange-looking cart with the two high wheels is an old clay cart. There are a couple of others at the far end of the pond."

"Down there, under water, all these years," she said musingly. "There's something eerie about it—as though a flood had caught them, just as the lava caught Pompeii."

I said, "No. The mules that drew the carts had long since gone to the soap factory, and the wheelwrights who shrunk the wide iron rims on the shoulder-high wheels were names on a churchyard stone before the water seeped in."

She said, "Just the same, there is something eerie about this place. I shall always remember it—think of it at night if ever I drive down this way."

I tried to laugh at her mood. There must be half a hundred such clay pits up and down the river. I could not see why this one should so impress her. Nor did I ask why she thought that she might be driving down this way some night.

But then I could not guess that this particular clay pit was the one upon which the attention of the whole valley would very soon be focused.

3

WE STARTED back toward River House. It was almost noon. I hadn't wasted a morning like this since the place had opened. But I didn't have the feeling that the morning had been wasted—rather I had the sense of standing on the verge of some momentous event.

On the way up the hill I said, "You were joking about breakfast, but I'm not joking about lunch. Can you?"

"Can I what?"

"Have lunch with me."

She said, "Why not? I told you that I wanted to see River House."

"All of it?"

"All of it," she said. Her smile was hardly a smile at all, yet I sensed there was laughter behind it. Not shared laughter, but laughter at my expense.

I tightened up a little inside. I could guess how the brush salesman with his foot in the door must feel when the housewife says that she doesn't really need any brushes, but she just might take a quick look. I wondered what the brush salesman did then—did he find himself a more likely prospect, or did he take a lopsided pride in his sales talk and move in for the kill?

We turned into the blue-graveled drive, found a space

to park and nothing more was said until we were inside. I ordered lunch without counting the house or wondering how big the noon throwaway would be. My mind was not on business. She was wearing a perfume that I had been aware of all morning and it seemed to me that I had never before been so completely aware of a woman.

She said, "You know, you've done surprisingly well in changing this place around—in spite of its being entirely commercial, the feeling of the past is still in this room."

"You aren't the first to say that, but you're the first who matters," I said.

She said, "I'm not teasing now. I meant that. I knew this house well in the old days and I've got the unreal feeling that these people lunching here today are guests."

Well, she had one advantage in appraising River House that I would never have—she had memory. I was going to take her on a tour of this place all right, as soon as we were finished with dessert, to see it through her eyes.

"Do you know," she said, "I'd especially like to see the upstairs."

I said, "There's nothing up there but my room. The rest of the rooms are used only for storage."

"I know," she said.

I didn't wonder how she knew.

"Let's do it now?" she said abruptly, stood up and started for the green-carpeted stairs. I followed her. I liked to watch her go up the stairs. She had fine, strong legs, with a good curve at the calf and a stout ankle. We stopped in front of the door at the top of the third flight of stairs and I opened the door and looked in. I made a move as though to let her precede me, assuming that she would step first to the window overlooking the river, as I had once or twice seen other girls do.

But she did not even cross the threshold. She stood looking in, and what she saw was a chest of drawers and

26

a bureau and a bed. There was a small desk and a steel filing cabinet against one wall and a small shelf of books.

"Books?" she said. "Do you like to read?" She studied the titles.

I said, "Whenever I get a little time."

She started to turn away. She said musingly, "I wanted to see where you lived. I hoped that it would tell me something about you. But it looks like a hotel room."

I said, "What else? This is a public house, not a home."

She swung a quick glance along the hall. "Shall we go down now?"

I put both hands on her shoulders. I turned her toward me, moving her so that her face was level with mine. But she put both hands against my chest, pushing.

"Not now," she said. "Not right here—not right now. These things can't be forced, not with me, at any rate."

I looked at her steadily, aware of a sincerity and a half-promise that were more important and more enticing than any other promise had been before.

I said, "Of course," and took my hands from her shoulders and touched her elbow, but only to guide her toward the stairs. I had waited before. I had waited through the war years and through most of the years since and now I had twisted life around a little, this past year or so, to fit a pattern I had long had in mind. The whole thing, the waiting, the planning, could have been upset in a matter of seconds here on the lonely third floor of River House.

She paused at the top of the stairs and looked at me. There was a skylight overhead and I could see the blue of her eyes and the question behind them—a question she seemed to be asking of herself, not me.

She smiled suddenly and said, "You're a patient man, Jason. I'm afraid of patient men. They don't often lose any game they play."

I said, "Then this is only a game?"

27

The smile went away. "No," she said slowly. "This isn't just a game any more. I thought you understood that." She turned quickly and started down the stairs.

When I had seen her out the front door to her car I asked, "Anne, if it isn't a game any more, will I see you tonight?"

She did not hesitate. "Of course," she said. "I'll come unescorted and you'll have to sit with me."

But I did not sit with her in the barroom of River House that night. I sat with a Major Craddock instead.

You might have been in the late great war and still have been lucky enough never to have met Major Craddock. He was not a combat soldier, nor yet stateside. He was—or had been—an MP officer. He had always operated in base section. Operated is the right word.

He came into the barroom at River House that Saturday night with his gut sucked in and his chest out and his shoulders very square. He had a crew cut and a big, blueish jaw. He kept his eyes squinted into dangerous slits, so there would be no doubt that, although here was a gentleman and upon occasion a very polished one, here, too, was a very hard case.

He came straight to the table where I sat waiting for Anne Cramer, and said, "You're Broome."

I put an inch of cigar ash into the black tray that had RIVER HOUSE printed on it in white letters. I leaned back in the caned chair and looked up at him.

I remembered this man, all right. One of his MP's had arrested me in a base section town for wearing a mixed uniform, minus a tie. I hadn't had much trouble proving why I was dressed that way. A phone call to a code number had fixed that. But the memory nudged me now and some of the old annoyance scratched across my palate. It made my voice raspy.

I said, "I'm Broome."

He sat down. He said, "Do you know who I am?"

I said, "No."

He said, "I am Major Craddock." His voice got a little smug. "I am General Gunther Cramer's right hand man."

I thought to myself, *You are just one shade removed from being General Gunther Cramer's dog-robber* . . . but I did not say that. I said, "How do you do, Major Craddock. I hope you are enjoying your stay in Newburyport."

He took out and lit a cigarette after frowning at my cigar. He went through all that silly business of tapping it and lighting it with great care.

He said, "Broome, I'm going to be blunt with you. It has come to the general's attention that his daughter has been seen in this place."

"Anything unusual about that?" I asked as casually as I could.

"No." He made a gesture with the manicured hand that held the king-size cigarette. "But the general doesn't like it. A little slumming is all right when it's done in a group, but not alone. I understand Miss Cramer has been here unescorted."

I felt the slow burn starting but I don't think it showed. I inhaled cigar smoke. It was heavy, rich and quieted my first angry impulses. I managed to say quietly enough, "My compliments to the general on the work of his intelligence agents. I hadn't thought of River House as a slum area."

The major thought that one over, changing color slightly. I got the feeling of an imminent explosion. When I looked down at his hands, all I could see were knuckles.

He said, "Look, Broome. Maybe I'd better use your own language. You've been putting up a big front here, but I know your background. I've looked you up. Do you begin to understand?"

I said, "No. I wear a clean shirt and don't swear in front

of ladies. Doesn't that make me a gentleman?"

"All right—crack wise. I've met a lot of men like you in my career. They're as brittle as their pretensions."

I said, "You're making me some kind of threat and I don't understand why."

I understood why all right, but I needed time. I needed to stall him. We were going to have it out—that was why he was here. The general probably said, "Craddock, my daughter is getting interested in a bum from the brickyards who runs some kind of a saloon out on Brickyard Avenue. Go take care of this bum."

The idea burned me, but under the burn it amused me a little, too. I wondered if the major still saluted the general. They were both out of the army but I would have bet they kept observing all the regulations.

"I'm not threatening you, Broome. I'm explaining a delicate situation. You are to discourage Anne's coming here. The general won't have it. Is that clear?"

I said, "You express yourself well, Major. If I don't give Anne Cramer the cold shoulder hereafter—I'm in serious trouble?"

He leaned back, relaxed. I could see the beginning of contempt and amusement in his eyes.

"I'm glad you realize that, Broome. I thought we would meet on common ground. I understand you had some sort of military experience yourself. You know how these things are."

I knew how they were. The army expected the corporal to be a better man than the private; and the majors and the bird-boys stood up in the officer's mess when the man with the star on his collar came in late. There was a reason for it, and a good one. A chain of command, unquestioning obedience, so automatic that it became a natural way of life in wartime.

But this was not war—not yet—and I didn't stand up any

more in the presence of field grade or better. I was a citizen of a free and democratic country and it was now my privilege to tell Major Craddock where to go.

I leaned across the table, even as he was relaxing, and told him just that. "Major Craddock, you can go to hell."

It might have been kinder to have hit him in the stomach. The result could have been no more startling. Craddock's neck began to swell and the fine, oxford collar cut into it and left a thin line of white, bloodless flesh in the midst of all that red flush of anger.

He got up at once, as I had expected he would, and the MP in him made his hand reach out automatically to take hold of my shirt front. I knew the next move. He would drag me up close and belt me across the mouth with the back of his other hand. I could imagine his arm and shoulder tensing under the expensive suit, preparing for just that effort.

I pushed my chair back quickly and walked to the door and he followed me, as I knew he would. I stepped out into the graveled drive and when he reached for me I took the sap out of my hip pocket and let it lie there across the palm of my hand where he could see it. The sap is a leather pouch, weighted with shot, the handle short but flexible. There was once a leather wrist thong on it, but I had cut that off.

I said, "You're bigger than I am, Major, and all things being equal you could beat me up. But all things are not equal, as you've just pointed out." I hefted the sap. I said, "I'm my own bouncer and this is only in case two people give me trouble at once. You're as big as two people. Were you thinking of giving me trouble?"

He didn't say anything for a minute. He looked the situation over. He wasn't afraid. I'm sure of that. He would have walked into me and taken the chance that I knew how to use that sap. But as angry as he was, there was a calculating glint in the depths of his squinted eyes. I couldn't actually see it there, but I could sense it.

He said, "Broome, you're a bigger fool than I thought you were. I could understand your having a gun, but not that sap. They never issue licenses for those things. It's a concealed weapon and you're not a police officer, and you have threatened me. You're in trouble, Broome."

"Why don't you go down to town, Major, and round up a couple of the boys in white helmets? Or don't the boys in white helmets recognize your rank any more?"

It didn't work. He said, "For a little while, Broome, I thought you might be going to be a problem. I overrated you. You're not any problem at all, now." He turned away and started across the gravel toward his car. It was a little satisfaction to me to see that I had guessed right about that— it was a fish-tail convertible, at least a five grand raytop, inelegantly. But that was about all the satisfaction that I did get from the incident.

I expected to hear from him again, but not quite the way it happened. The next I heard of him, Major Craddock was dead.

I went back into the barroom after Major Craddock had left. It was Saturday night, the big night of the week at River House. At the bar I told Armando to give me Black Label. I swallowed the drink down fast. He had the chaser ready but I shook my head and gave him back the empty shot glass and he filled it again. I never drink more than two in succession like that and although I wanted a third, I walked away from the bar without it.

My date with Anne Cramer was obviously off for tonight. And yet it didn't seem reasonable to me that the general, or Major Craddock either, could dictate to Anne. I had not given much thought to her age, but it seemed quite apparent that she had been long enough out of school to be well-started down her twenties. She was a free agent, an adult. Wasn't there a chance that she might ignore her father and come anyway?

As I moved around the room, never quite sure to whom I was speaking, I had one eye on the door. But Anne Cramer did not put in an appearance, nor did I see anything more of Major Craddock.

At closing time I walked with the last of the guests to the blue drive. When the parking lot was empty, I went back inside and got the cash deposit bag and went around to my own car. I gave the motor a half-minute to warm up, wondering if I was making a mistake to go down to the bank alone at this hour of the night. I wonder about it every Saturday night, though nothing has ever happened. Newburyport has a good and efficient police department.

I cut off Brickyard Avenue into Water Street and slowed to the legal limit. Prowl cars often cruised here. I saw a couple of drunks rolling home, and a girl too young for what she was doing leaned out from the curb and made an elaborate pick-up gesture. I grinned at her and went on, but when I stopped in front of the bank and went over to the bronze plate of the night depository she hurried along the street and stopped beside me.

"You look lonesome, honey," she said. "Ain't nothing worse than being lonesome at this hour."

Her dress was a sleazy thing with a transparent upper half that showed a white brassiere and lots of flesh beneath it. She stood on spikes too high for her, and her smile was a brittle mask, covering her youth and inexperience.

I said, "Kid, you ought to be home in bed."

She giggled. "Let's you and me make a night of it."

Jailbait, maybe. It was hard to tell the age under that mask of powder, rouge and mascara. I had seen too many

33

like her on the *Via Roma*. It bothered me that it could happen here.

I made my deposit and turned back. "Broke, kid?"

She pulled her dress up and there was a wad of bills in the top of her stocking. "What do you think?"

I might have come up with a fin to pay her to take herself out of my way quickly, but just then we both heard the car coming. The red light on the roof wasn't flashing and the siren was stilled but we could both see the lettering: POLICE.

She said, "I'll see you at the foot of the block," and dodged down River Street. I shook my head and crossed to my car. The prowl wagon went past, both cops turning for a brief look But a man making a night deposit was a common enough sight along Water Street.

I drove back toward Brickyard Avenue and River House, wondering about the girl, about her home life, about how she got that way. My thoughts were impersonal, detached. I decided idly that probably it had been fortunate for me that the police had come along just when they did—they had saved me a fin and the trouble of getting rid of the girl . . .

How was I to know that Major Craddock was dead by now and that a good, sweet alibi was all ready to cover me— or would have been, if two cops hadn't come down Water Street past the bank at three-thirty on a Sunday morning and seen me talking to a tart?

4

IT WAS past four in the morning when I got out to River House. I took a shower, had a drink from the upstairs bottle, and went to bed thinking about Anne and the major and wondering just how tough the latter would be. I got some sleep but not enough. A steady thumb on the downstairs bell button brought me up in a hurry to an awareness of daylight.

I crossed foggily to the window. A gray Ford and a red Nash stood in the parking lot out front and I came awake fast. That's a combination that spells trouble in our township. The state police drive gray Fords. The sheriff drives a red Nash.

I went across the room to where I had folded my pants across the back of a chair. I took the blackjack out of the hip pocket, shoved it in a dresser drawer, and went downstairs and through the lower hall to the door. Three men stood outside, a state trooper, the sheriff, and some man whom I didn't know by sight, but whom I found out later to be a D.A.'s investigator.

I opened the door and said, "Yes?" and waited.

They didn't say anything. They just walked in.

Sheriff Ehrets I knew by sight. He is still a reasonably young man, under fifty, I'd guess; but he has a shock of white hair. As far as I knew he was a quiet, unobtrusive official, not given to using his authority without reason. But when something happened outside the orbit of the city police department, he usually went along with the state troopers.

Now he said, "You're Jason Broome?"

"That's right."

"Do you know a Major Craddock?"

I nodded. I supposed that Craddock had gone to the police about my having threatened him. Yet it hardly seemed reasonable that a complaint like that would bring out so much police authority on a Sunday morning. I suppose that it was just about then that I started to suspect that something really serious might have happened, but of course I had no idea what, or, above all, why.

"I know him," I said.

"You knew him," the sheriff said. "Make it past tense. Craddock is dead. Do you want to put on some clothes before you come along with us?"

I said, "Why would I be going along with you? I'm not under arrest, am I?"

Ehrets said mildly, "Not exactly. But some stories have come into the D.A.'s office this morning, stories that make it necessary for us to question you. As far as we know you run a legitimate place out here and you've never been in trouble. I even recall that you had a good war record. So we'll make it as easy on you as we can. Just some questions. You understand?"

I said, "Yeah, I guess I do." I didn't, of course, but thought it best to play along. He was right about my never having been in trouble, and I didn't want to start now. "I'll go upstairs and get dressed. I suppose you'll want to come along."

Ehrets only nodded and he and the state trooper and the D.A.'s man followed me up the stairs.

The room was a little crowded with them all standing

there. Ehrets went over to the window and said, "Nice view. I always wanted one of those cabin cruisers." He watched the small boat out on the river cut a faint wake on the wide, blue expanse of water. The other two didn't pay any attention. I saw the D.A.'s man looking at my bookshelf—he was appraising everything in the room with surprising thoroughness.

The trooper wasn't interested in anything. He was just there in case I wanted to get tough, I supposed, and because—I suddenly realized—the state police needed to be represented in the arrest of a murder suspect.

That jolted me. So Craddock's death was murder—and I was a suspect. But not enough of a suspect as yet to have been placed officially under arrest.

I went on dressing silently and nobody said anything. After a while we all trooped downstairs and I got into the red car with Ehrets. We started toward town, the gray car almost nosing our bumper all the way.

The court house is an old building, in the middle of a green square. It is nicely shaded and somehow reminiscent of a summer vacation scene on a Saratoga Springs postcard. I must have passed it a thousand times in my life and never given it more than a brief glance. This morning I did. This bright, warm summer Sunday morning, in the office of the district attorney, I found myself thinking of all the grim business of law that went on behind these clean white walls— and of how it might pertain to me especially.

A church bell started its Sunday summons—from not far away, a carillon chimed in. There was sunlight and shadow outside the window and I could smell new-mown grass. It was Sunday in the country with pot roast waiting on the stove. But first there would be services. Boys in clean shirts and girls in dresses that looked summery walked side by side toward church entrances; and even if they were laughing and giggling on the sidewalks, they were solemn as they approached the doors but not half so solemn as I.

District Attorney Thomas E. Welsh was a tall thin man with glasses. He looked troubled and mildly annoyed, as though the thought of spending a Sunday morning in an office that smelled of jail disinfectant, of leather bindings on law books, of oiled sweeping compound and cigars smoked long ago, was not his idea of a pleasant time. either.

He was writing in a looseleaf notebook when we came into the room and beside the desk sat a young man, a little stout, dressed in slacks and sport shirt. He had put a checked sports jacket over the back of his chair, for it was getting warm. He looked up and nodded to the trooper, stood up and followed the latter out into the hall. They talked in low tones and the trooper went away. The stout young man came back and I guessed that he was from the B.C.I.—the local Bureau of Criminal Investigation. We had a full house.

The district attorney finished writing, leaned back and looked at me across the desk. The man who had been introduced as the D.A.'s investigator went around and sat at the end of the desk opposite the B.C.I. man. I don't know what Ehrets did—he remained behind me, somewhere, out of sight. I heard the door of the office close.

I stood there facing the other three, thinking how much they looked like three judges. I felt something touch the backs of my legs and Ehrets said, "Sit down."

I said, "Thanks," and sat down in the chair he pushed under me.

The district attorney said, "Broome, you've had a good reputation until last night. At least no one ever indicated otherwise, so far as the police can tell. What prompted you to turn wrong all of a sudden? Why the threat against Major Craddock?"

I still didn't know from where he had his information, and I certainly didn't want to answer that last question. There was only one thing that I did want at the moment. I wanted a lawyer. But it seemed cowardly and a little stupid of me not to be able to account for myself without having my lawyer at my elbow.

I said, "You seem to have picked up a lot of information in a short space of time. I hope you can assess it at its true value."

Welsh didn't say anything to that, but his investigator leaned forward and said, "Don't get funny and don't get tough, Broome. This isn't any third degree stuff. We're paid to do a job and we're doing it. You admit that you had a quarrel with Major Craddock last night?"

I thought about that. I said, "That's right."

"You threw him out of the bar at River House?"

"Not physically. But I was prepared to."

"Would you care to tell us the reason for the disagreement?"

I said, "It couldn't possibly have any bearing on whatever happened to him later. It wasn't that kind of a quarrel."

"Was he disorderly? Drunk?"

"No. We disagreed on a personal matter."

The district attorney interrupted. "You can have a lawyer if you so desire, Broome. You understand that we are asking you questions that might bring forth answers that could be used against you?"

"I understand that," I said. "I'm assuming Major Craddock was killed or met with an accident last night, after he and I had a quarrel. I don't know how you found that out, but it's true. I'll make it a statement of further fact. I never saw Major Craddock again after he drove away."

The sheriff, standing somewhere behind me said, "Are you sure you don't want to call your lawyer?"

I said, "Not yet, thanks. I don't think I need a lawyer. I had a quarrel with the major. He drove away. That's all I know. What else can I tell you? I don't know anything else about it. I don't even know how he died."

The B.C.I. man said, "You understand that we can hold you for carrying a concealed, unlicensed weapon?"

"The blackjack?" I said. "So Craddock told you. Well, I'm my own bouncer out at River House. I don't have much trouble. It's a respectable place. But when I first opened, some hoodlums dropped in. One of them pulled that blackjack on me when I tried to put them out. I took it away from him. I've kept it since as a souvenir. I can bring witnesses to testify how I came by it—and I don't think you can get a conviction."

The B.C.I. man did not seem disturbed. He said mildly, "That's about the way of it. I suppose half the night business places have a blackjack or a club lying around handy. What makes your case different is that you carried that sap outside the building. You threatened a man with it, and we have a complaint on the records about that. The man who made the complaint was killed after he made the complaint— by a blow at the base of the skull."

If he had been excited, or yelled, or threatened me, I might have got up enough steam to fight back. But he laid it on the line so calmly, with such deadly sureness that I sat back in the chair and began to wonder which of the local lawyers would do me the most good.

I said, "When was Major Craddock killed? What time, I mean?"

The district attorney's investigator said, "Under the evidence, so far, isn't it reasonable to assume that you might be able to tell us that?"

I didn't say anything and the B.C.I. man said, "If you're thinking that you have several witnesses to prove that you were in the barroom until three o'clock closing, that won't help."

I said, "Then it was after three? Between three and four?"

The D.A. said, "You make that sound like a question. You're sure it's not a statement?"

I said, "No. It's not a statement." I wished to be the hell out of that hot little office and into the cool and pleasant morning air. But I had no particular anger at these men for what they were trying to do. I could even appreciate the spot they were on. They had a murder case on their hands and no matter how you looked at it, I was the most likely suspect. I had had motive, opportunity—even the weapon.

I said, "If you're so damned sure I'm guilty, why didn't one of your men ask me for the blackjack when you picked me up? Why didn't you search my place for it? If I'd used it to kill a man, your lab experts could tell you."

The B.C.I. man said, "We don't know what you used. We haven't even accused you—yet. No warrants have been served up to now. We're simply asking for your cooperation."

What bothered me was the feeling I had that they were sure. They could afford to be calm and reasonable, if withdrawn and hardfaced and contemptuous under the courtesy. The thing must have looked easy from where they sat.

I said, "Where was the body found? Or is that one of the questions I'm supposed to answer?"

After a glance at the D.A. the B.C.I. man said, "In the clay pit, down at the brickyard."

I said, "How did it get there? By car?" I wished I hadn't said that ten seconds after I said it, but it was too late then.

"That's right," the B.C.I. man said. "At dawn this morning we took a cast of the tire marks. We checked your tires before we rang your bell this morning. We concede that the treads don't match."

I said, "Then what are you holding me for?"

"You might have borrowed a car."

I said, "I didn't borrow a car." I was acutely aware at that moment of having been at the clay pit yesterday with Anne Cramer. In Anne's car.

I was going to tell them next about going to the bank. I

41

had remembered the girl who had stopped and talked to me, and the police car coming by and the girl running down the side street and the cops turning to look at me, but going on. I was wondering if the time element there would help me—if the city police themselves might have the alibi for me that I so desperately needed. But just then there was a knock at the door.

The sheriff opened it and I could tell by the expressions on the three faces opposite me that something very unusual had happened.

I turned to look, and Anne Cramer was standing there. She said to all of us in general, "May I come in?" and came in without waiting for permission. When the sheriff made no move to shut the door, she reached out and shut it herself.

There was an awkward little pause and, because this was police business, I suppose, no one stood up. Finally Ehrets pushed another chair forward and Anne sat down.

If District Attorney Welsh was annoyed, he didn't show it. After all, his was an elective office and Anne Cramer was known to him. More important, her father, General Gunther Cramer, was known to him, too. But he had to do something as a token of respect for the law he had sworn to uphold.

He said, "Miss Cramer, this is a small private session—a sort of unofficial investigation. I'm sure you didn't realize that when you came in. If there is something you wanted to see me about, I'll be glad to talk to you later."

She looked around the room, at the B.C.I. man, and the D.A.'s investigator and finally at the sheriff. She looked at everyone but me. Then she said, "This is all a matter that concerns the death of Major Craddock, isn't it? I heard about it—never mind how. I also heard that the district attorney was questioning a suspect. That's why I came right down here."

"Do you know the suspect?" Welsh asked.

"I know him very well." Anne lowered her gaze when she said that and right then I got an inkling of what might be coming next and started to sweat in earnest. I hoped she knew what she was doing. I was trying to get my own alibi shaped up in my own mind—the police, and the scene in front of the bank at three-thirty or thereabouts. If she wasn't careful she might step on that and we'd both be in worse trouble.

Welsh said, "Then am I to assume that your presence here has some bearing on the matter at hand?"

She was obviously nervous. She seemed quite pale, but that could have been part of the act. No make-up perhaps. I wasn't sure. But I was sure about the way her tongue tried to moisten lips obviously gone dry. She had a handkerchief in her hand and her fingers were busy with it. I heard a definite tearing sound.

"That's why I came down at once," she said. "I knew that Jason would allow himself to be brought into court before he would talk. I think—I believe—that he would go to the chair rather than tell the truth."

The D.A. said, "Then are we to assume, Miss Cramer, that you have come here voluntarily to offer us some help? You have some information that you wish to give us?"

She said, "Can what I say here be kept secret?"

"This isn't a grand jury room, Miss Cramer. On the other hand—none of the press are present. And knowing you, and your family position in the community, I think it safe to say that anything you may have to tell us will be confidential until such time as it might serve the ends of justice for it to be made public."

We all saw the faint tremor of her shoulders. She took a deep breath and lifted her head. She said, "I am not asking that you be lenient in your judgment of me, or of my actions —but it is the nature of your office that you should want to see justice done, and there would be no justice in your holding Jason. He had no opportunity to commit this crime."

"You seem quite certain, Miss Cramer."

"I am certain. I was waiting for him to close at River House last night. We went upstairs together. He did not leave his room until he came down to my car with me—at dawn."

The district attorney sat back in his chair. Its swivel squeaked.

He said, "You would swear to this on the witness stand?"

"If I had to, yes—regardless of the consequences."

No one said anything for seconds and I supposed that was because there did not seem to be much to say. The feel of embarrassment was as heavy as the heat in the room. But it must have been my own embarrassment for none of the others seemed especially shocked. It occurred to me that in police work a great deal of this sort of thing must come out—shoddy passions, assignations, regardless of caste.

Only the D.A.'s investigator seemed to have a question to ask. He leaned forward, his eyes hating us. He said, "Miss Cramer, did you happen to notice any of the furnishings of Broome's bedroom? Were there any wall decorations, such as paintings? Or books?"

She looked at him very steadily. She said, "There were some books on a wall shelf. I can't remember all of the titles. *Cakes and Ale* was one. That's by Maugham, isn't it? Then there was a kind of circus book. *Chad Hanna*, I think. And I remember that there was a novel about the Hudson Valley by Brick. I've read that one. There were some paperbacks, too. I can't remember the titles. Yes I can, too—one was a reprint, not an original edition. *From Here To Eternity*. I remember the movie."

The D.A.'s investigator lifted his shoulders briefly and then let them regain their normal slouch. He made an open gesture with his hands, expressive of defeat. I remember his studying that bookshelf while they waited for me to dress that morning. I suspected now that he was a good man at his job, also a suspicious man. But that gesture with the hands—that was surrender.

They all stood up, so I stood up too. The district attorney said to me, "I regret any inconvenience that we may have caused you." He turned to Anne. He said, "It took a definite courage to do what you have just done, Miss Cramer. I hope that you will be rewarded for it. Good day, ma'm. You are both free to go."

The sheriff opened the door of the office. It was cooler in the corridor. We walked toward the wide doorway and there was a breeze. We stood at the top of the steps. We could hear voices, singing voices, from the church across the street. It was still only Sunday morning.

I said, "Anne, why did you lie about last night?"

She looked around. No one was near us. She said, "I couldn't let them blame you, Jason."

"But if they put you on the witness stand—"

"They won't," she said. "They know they can't break me down." That strength again—the touch of her shoulder. The feel of her in my arms.

We started down the court house steps. I said, "Anne, let me take you to lunch." I was a little dizzy with the nearness of her—the idea of lunch after what we had just been through seemed inane and irrelevant. But suddenly I didn't want to lose her, not for some moments at least.

"I can't go to lunch with you," she said. "The general needs me."

The general needed her. Not her father, but the general. The fact that he was also her father was secondary. I remembered everything that I had tried to forget about the army caste system.

We stopped at the curb and I opened the door of the green Mercury. She slid under the wheel and smiled up at me.

"But I will see you again soon?" I said hopefully.

45

"As soon as I can get away. And don't look so worried. Everything will be all right now."

I watched her drive away. And then it hit me. Don't look so worried. I had an alibi now, and so had she. I was her alibi.

I suppose I knew at that moment that Anne had killed Major Craddock as surely as any gossip ever would, and that she was using me as always she would use anyone she needed at a given moment. I knew, and didn't know—and certainly chose not to believe.

5

WHEN Anne drove away and left me standing at the curb it was several seconds before I remembered that I did not have my car. There was a supermarket near the court house and sometimes it was possible to find a taxi waiting there. But it was Sunday—the parking lot was vacant. I thought I had better walk across the village to the railroad station rather than go back inside the court house to phone for a cab.

It seems as though all the villages and towns and cities along the Hudson slope down to the river. Our village is no exception. As I started walking toward the railroad station I felt a natural tendency to start running; yet I remembered from childhood that when one started running toward the river it was difficult to stop.

I thought I had better curb that tendency to start running—I had better walk carefully and thoughtfully with the knowledge I had.

I strode through the business section, past a meat market and a grocery, a hat store and a clothing store, and that brought to mind the general's building boom. He had seen it coming, and his development company was building a whole new housing project on the outskirts of town. The whole community was benefiting.

47

I thought about the inevitable influx of outsiders and tried to link it with Craddock's death, with Anne. No, not with Anne. The general had his own construction company and brought many of his workers to this new project from completed jobs elsewhere around the country. He might have had trouble with one of them and Craddock had been his whip. But nothing like that had ever happened here, and I couldn't believe it had now.

I stopped and looked in a store window. I couldn't tell you what the merchant had for sale. I kept seeing a face that was not my own.

Not even Anne's.

It was a man's face. It was the thin, tired face of the district attorney's investigator, whose name was Ray Hoyle. The man had impressed me. There had been nothing spectacular or even forceful about him. But he had seemed as necessary to the decor of the court house as the scales of justice. I suspect a lot of people thought of him as nemesis.

I thought of him now as a menace to Anne.

You've read about a chill up and down the spine. I had that, in spite of the summer heat. I shook it off at once. My own guilt complex was busy. I hadn't killed the major. But when Anne had come along with the alibi that I hadn't deserved, I hadn't called her on it.

Now, who was whose alibi? I was back to that again— knowing, yet not believing.

Then what had been bothering me popped to the surface again. I stood still and looked into a show window and concentrated. I got it.

What if Hoyle found out that I had been talking to a girl on Water Street between three-thirty and four in the morning? If Hoyle was the thinker he seemed to be, he had possibly already got around to thinking about Saturday night being a big night in a ginmill—and someone going to the bank with the locked cash bag. He might even be out at River House already, asking discreet questions.

Armando would rise to the sight of a badge, a suggestion of robbery. "We're way ahead of you, mister. The boss always goes down after closing to make a night deposit." Armando was proud that his boss was brave enough not to ask police protection.

I started toward the cab stand at the railroad station. When the hackie pulled up at River House, Armando was getting ready to open.

"Hi, boss," he said. "You're the first customer in the bar today."

I said, "Look kid—did you go straight home last night?"

"Are you kiddin', boss? Would I be hanging around a bottle club after hours? I mean, after all, last night was the big one, and me on my aching feet for hours—"

I said, "I'm not kidding. Will you do me a favor?"

"Within reason, boss. Anything up to murder. A married man has to draw the line somewhere."

I fed it to him hard. I said, "It is murder, Armando. But it's already committed and I didn't have any part of it. I had a quarrel with Major Craddock last night. Kind of a public quarrel, as you know. By the way—has anybody been here asking questions?"

"No, boss."

I said, "Good. I didn't kill Craddock."

"Who says you did?"

"Nobody says so outright. But some people down at the court house think I might have."

"You say you didn't. That makes it all right with me."

"Thanks, Armando. Now get this. I can prove where I was at the time of the murder. Except that somebody who saw me make a deposit, or later checks on the fact that I did make a deposit, can shoot that proof full of holes."

You don't have to spell it out in large, simple letters for

Armando. He said, "So I made the deposit on my way home. It ain't perjury unless I swear to it, is it?"

I said, "No, and you won't have to swear to it. If a man comes out here and asks you, you made the deposit—because I had a date. Upstairs. He'll go away and you'll never have to swear to it."

He said to me, "Do you hear a rumbling noise, boss?"

I said, "No. Why?"

He said, "When I walk on thin ice I always hear a rumbling noise." He stood there, polishing a glass, and listened to his private sounds. Anyone who didn't know him might have thought that Armando was waiting for me to make a bid. But I knew Armando. You couldn't buy from Armando what I needed. It had to come as a gift. I waited.

A car drove up out front—it might have been a party arriving for the late lunch hour, but it wasn't. It was Hoyle, the D.A.'s man. The closeness of his timing made me feel a little sick. I still didn't have Armando's answer. I slipped out the back way and took a walk in the woods. Let Hoyle think I was still in town.

There is a stream that runs down through the woods in back of River House. It widens out into a glade and someone, before my time, had made a sort of garden down there. I sat down and lit a cigar. I chewed on the end to get it to draw better and spat out a piece of tobacco with force.

I had been trying to think like a fox but I had been running like a rabbit. Now I would have to sit here and wait and think some more. There wasn't anything more to think about, as far as Hoyle was concerned. He had his last chance; his only chance now was to trip me up. I wondered how he was making out.

I had to think about something else, for the suspense was piling up in me. The fact that it happened to be a very special sort of a summer's day made the tension all the harder to take.

The thought of Anne Cramer seemed like a good antidote for the poison that was filling me, so I thought of Anne Cramer. I would have to begin, sooner or later, to find a better reason than the obvious one for her having shamed herself in the presence of a group of law officers. I thought— and the idea shook me as nothing ever had—of her being in love with me, and discovered that I wanted to believe that.

The full impact of our relationship didn't really hit me until this moment when I sat there alone in a summer garden thinking about her. Except for her statement I might now be under twenty-four hour custody with charges pending—but this wasn't what was stepping up my pulse at the moment. I was remembering the way she had made her statement. Not boldly, or in defiance, or even in any sort of shame-faced desperation. She had simply made it a quiet and casual statement of fact as though it were the most natural thing in the world that she had spent the night at River House. I wondered if her explanation had come so easily because she had indeed considered such a possibility —had in fact been heading toward it from the moment that she had stumbled and come into my arms down on the flats by the old barge?

Yet that very noon she had held me at arm's length—what had she said? *"These things can't be forced, not with me . . ."* and *"You're a patient man, Jason. Patient men don't often lose any game they play . . ."* What did I know about women? Perhaps she had made up her mind to lose right then, and her "confession" this morning had been a prediction . . .

She loved me, I thought—she *must.*

I got up and started back toward the barroom. I had reached my conviction—I didn't want to reason it out any more. Perhaps it was wishful thinking—or perhaps I had realized a dream.

51

Just to be different I went around to the front of River House. The barroom was open now and I walked in the front door. I had already seen that Hoyle's car was gone. I walked over to the bar. The rush that always follows the opening of the bar was well under way and Armando was a very busy man. I sat down at the far end of the bar and waited. It was dim in here and the cut-glass on the back bar picked up what little light there was and shredded it down to a living filigree of incandescence.

I stared at the quivering lines of light in the cut-glass flagons, watching them twitch and reshape, and suddenly Armando stood in front of me with a bottle of Johnny Walker in his hand and said in a voice that reached only my ears, "Did I meet anyone in front of the bank last night?"

I looked at him and thought that his hand wasn't as steady as it usually was. I said, "There was a dame on the make. Flimsy blouse, skirt, wobbly heels. A police car came along and she ducked down River Street."

Armando said, "A tart, huh? My word is as good as hers. Hoyle asked me did I see anybody and I said there was some dames around, sure. There always is, on a Saturday night down there. I see in the paper last week where one of the dumb clucks tried to pick up a plainclothes-cop and got tossed in the can."

I said, "You used your head. When the prowl car went past they didn't see my face. Not well, anyhow. We're about the same build, and I'm glad that you liked my mustache well enough to grow the one you're wearing."

He touched it, brushing it down with the little finger of his right hand. I took the drink he offered me.

I said, "'You're all right, Armando. I guess I always knew that."

His shrug was a masterpiece. He went away to the other end of the bar. I thought, *Damn that Hoyle* . . . He had pretty near trapped me—both Anne and me. But it looked now as

though we had him stopped. I couldn't picture him inter-
viewing every tart in town—and I was sure that the police
hadn't had too good a look at me. They would have to pick
me out of a line-up which would also include Armando. I
didn't think they could do it.

I sat there at the bar and lit a cigarette for a change.
There was a hum of conversation through the room and
suddenly I was listening without seeming to or even meaning to. And from the conversation I got more news about
Major Craddock's death.

The story of his disappearance had been on the early-
morning news broadcast of the local radio station. A woman
who lived in a house up the road from the old brickyard—
one of the old-timers who had refused to leave the once-
prosperous area—had noticed a car at the clay pit during
the night. Its lights had awakened her. She had stood for
a time at the open window without seeing much. Perhaps
she had had an old person's interest in what she had
thought was the carrying-on of a wild, younger generation.
But there had been some unusual sound—a splashing, perhaps—and the car had raced away soon thereafter.

The woman had noticed the time. It had been shortly
after four o'clock. This had raised some further question
in her mind. She was a retired schoolteacher and trained to
reason matters through to a conclusion. At first she might
have suspected that she had merely witnessed a Saturday
night romp of the younger generation. But when she heard
on the early-morning broadcast that Major Craddock had
disappeared, it had seemed worth while to her to call the
state police.

Within ten minutes after their arrival in the abandoned
brickyard, the state police had found Major Craddock's
body. Apparently someone had intended to sink the major
out of sight forever. But they had not reckoned on the
location of a dead crabapple tree fully awash in the north

end of the pit. The major's body had snagged on the submerged tree branches. It had been easily spotted by the first state trooper who looked into the pit.

This much of the story came to me simply from listening. I asked no questions. I hardly needed to. I could see the pattern. The major had left me, to go direct to the state police and make a complaint that I had tried to sap him. That explained why I had been picked up for questioning so soon after the body was found.

Sitting there at the bar I shivered a little, thinking about it. If Anne Cramer hadn't come to my rescue I would be in a bad jam right now. Not that I wasn't still in trouble. Hoyle's coming out to River House so soon after my release proved that fact. Maybe I was building Hoyle up too much. Maybe Hoyle wasn't the dogged, persevering character that I thought he was. But so far he had lived up to expectations.

A business man whom I knew casually was seated two stools away. When he glanced over and nodded I said, "Craddock's death seems to be the big topic today. Have they picked up anyone for questioning?"

"Not a soul, so far. I've heard every broadcast today. The police seemed to be up against a stone wall from the start."

So they hadn't mentioned my name on any of the broadcasts. No one here in this room now, no one in town except those directly involved, knew that I had been taken in and questioned. And from that fact came a new question and a new doubt.

If my name hadn't been released, if no broadcast so far today had mentioned me—how had Anne Cramer known that I was in custody: And how long would it take Ray Hoyle to want an answer to that question?

Since I had first met Anne Cramer, she had been constantly in my mind. I had wanted to be with her more than with any other woman I had known. It was almost as if every detail of her physical and spiritual makeup had instantly imprinted itself upon my subconscious mind—as with someone you've known forever. And suddenly it became urgent, even imperative, that I see her again.

How had she known that I was in custody?

I left the bar and went over and sat down at my usual table. I watched the door. Yesterday she had come, but today I had the feeling that she would not. She had been in too much of a hurry to get away from me earlier at the court house.

I knew where her home was. It was here on the hill above the brickyards. I could go out and get my car and drive a half mile up Brickyard Avenue toward Newburyport, make a right turn and three minutes later hit the gateposts to the Cramer estate. But that was as far as I would get. The gateposts.

It wasn't hard to remember the contempt in Craddock's voice when he had told me that the general didn't want Anne coming to River House—or associating with me. But now I asked myself was it—had it been—the general's wish that Anne have nothing at all to do with me, or Craddock's.

I got up, crossed over to the bar and, under cover of having another drink, told Armando that I was going out. I didn't tell him where I was going or what time I would be back.

He looked at me steadily. "If you're going to see the girl, be careful. I've heard some rumors that before he died, Craddock sent for some of his old buddies. They were coming to town because of the danger of some trouble with the general's contractors. But now with the major dead—"

I understood exactly what he meant. A man like Craddock could be counted on to know some goons. But it seemed very important to me now that I reach Anne at once, and the only way to do that was to go where Anne was. I told Armando that I would certainly be careful of anyone I met. I went out and got my car and drove up the road to the lane that branched off toward the Cramer home.

It was a secondary road but well cared for. I made good time. When I reached the gateposts I was surprised to see that no one was there. The gatehouse itself had an unused look. I turned the car up the drive. I was expecting almost anything to happen, except what did happen. I had hardly stopped the car when two men about my own age came down the white steps.

One of them came around and leaned on the door on my side of the car. His friend was looking in at me from the side nearest the house. I had the feeling of being in the middle and didn't like it.

"Whom did you want to see?" the first one asked.

"I'd like to see Anne," I said.

"You're a friend of hers?" the man nearest to me asked.

The other one said across the empty seat beside me, "He looks to me like another newspaperman. The press isn't welcome out here right now. The general will issue a release when he's damned good and ready, not before. You're not going to kick this thing into a big story just because the major lived here."

I thought that it was remarkable how much a man could learn by letting someone else do all the talking. I said, "I'm not a reporter. I'm a friend of the family." That was stretching it a little, but I thought that it sounded like the right approach. It wasn't.

"Yeah?" The man standing nearest to me looked over at his companion.

The man on the far side of the car said, "We've heard that story a dozen times today. I'll call the butler. He'll know you."

56

I said, "Wait a minute—Anne'll know me."

They both laughed.

"We can't," the man across the car from me said. "She's gone in to the undertaker's to make arrangements for the major's funeral."

I said, "Has the coroner released the body so soon? What were the final results of the autopsy?"

Neither of them laughed now. They looked extremely sober.

"You ask a lot of questions," the one on my side of the car said. "Why don't you go away and come back later? Leave your name. We'll see that Miss Anne gets the message."

I thought about that. That "Miss Anne" suggested hired hands—yet these two were too well dressed to be servants. The late Major Craddock's goonboys? Craddock had been an operator, and these two looked the part in an even more sinister way. I wondered what use the general had for them—or they for him.

I said, "Tell Anne that Jason Broome called, will you?"

They said, "Broome?" together as though they might have rehearsed it that way.

I dropped the shift lever into drive and put a little gas to the motor. I started to move. I said, "I'll be seeing you."

I could see them in the rear-view mirror as I drove away. They were looking after me. I'd be seeing them again, I thought. The question was where—and how soon?

6

I GOT my answer that night. When I woke up alone in River House, the dial of the clock on the bureau said that it was ten minutes past two in the morning. Someone was moving around downstairs.

I lay there for a half-minute or so wondering what to do. What with one thing and another, I hadn't bothered making my nightly drop-off at the bank. Someone might have noticed that. But I didn't think so. I had made quite a production of trying to get in touch with Anne during the evening. I had even phoned and not got through to her. It seemed at least possible that someone intended that I didn't get through to her, then or possibly ever again.

I went to the closet and took a .22 rifle out from behind my trench coat. It was loaded.

I picked it up and carried it the way you carry a carbine. I wished now that it was a carbine. A .22 rifle will stop a man only if he is easily frightened.

I picked up a flashlight from the dresser, opened the door and went to the head of the stairs. I could hear my own sharp breathing, and tried to tone it down. I held the .22 in front of me, flashlight clamped to its barrel, my thumb on the switch.

There wasn't a sound from downstairs now. I wondered

58

if I had been dreaming. Next I wondered with a kind of panicky wishfulness if it could be Anne down there. No nice girl would come calling on a man in the middle of the night—but no nice girl will confess to having spent a night with a man, either, just to save him from the chair. A very lovely girl might though, and Anne was lovely.

Then, suddenly, in the darkness of the stairwell I heard the faintest sound of a stumble and a man's voice cursed. Quickly another voice said "Shut up!" In the dark, unseeing, I linked the voices to faces that I had seen that afternoon at Cramer's.

Friends of Major Craddock.

I knew a cold, uncertain feeling. If there had been two break-in artists down there come to work on the office safe there would have been a sort of pattern to what they were doing and I would have known the appropriate move to make. Even if they had been a couple of neighborhood hoodlums after cigarettes and liquor there would have been a pattern to their actions and I could have met it as I had met such things before.

But the two friends of Major Craddock's were something else. I had recognized them that afternoon as professional hardcases. Sometimes it seems to me that there is nothing more tragic than a professional badman, unless it is two professional badmen. I had met them in the army, I had met them overseas, and whatever their color, creed or nationality, they always came to the same end. But until they reached that end, they were dangerous.

I still didn't know what these two wanted—I decided to wait it out.

It came to me after a while that they were in no hurry. If they had come here after me, they were evidently familiarizing themselves with the downstairs setup, perhaps with some idea of a quick retreat. It made sense, I thought—

Major Craddock must have trained his boys well. The military mind at work.

But why should I mean anything to them—why should they have come here after me? Almost immediately one answer presented itself—perhaps they thought, as did the police, that I had knocked off their major? If they thought so, and if they had depended on Craddock, then the code of their kind was plain.

But who could have told them about me—unless it was Anne? I swore silently and felt my hands begin to sweat. I gripped the .22 harder.

There was no doubt in my mind about my legal right to do what I was going to have to do. There was not even any doubt about my moral right. And thinking back to it, I am even sure that I had no personal doubt of success. I was on familiar ground. I was the householder—everything was in my favor, with one exception.

I had grown away from violence. A weapon no longer came naturally to my hand. In a moment of quick rage I might revert to violence, but there was no quick rage within me yet—I did not even know what I was fighting. All I could go on was conjecture.

They started up the stairs at last and one said to the other, "Quiet, will you? Want to wake him up?"

The other voice said, "He'll wake up when we get to him. What's the difference?"

I was standing at the head of the stairs. I could see vague silhouettes.

I said, "This is the difference," and, without turning on the beam of the flashlight, squeezed off a shot. I hoped to place it between the feet of the first man—at the worst I would strike him only in the leg or foot.

They swore, both of them, all in one voice it seemed, as though they had rehearsed it that way. They made quick, awkward, stumbling sounds on the stairs. The sounds were those of retreat. They were withdrawing in a hurry. But to how far away? I remembered how carefully they had reconnoitered the first floor.

I waited, heard the front door open and turned to the open window. A car came alive on the blue drive and when it pulled away, I saw it was a Buick convertible I had not noticed around before. The top was down and two men were in the car. They drove away fast.

For a minute I felt nothing but relief, born perhaps of my association with the law that morning—born of the fact that I did not have to call the police to tell them that this time I *had* killed a man.

I stood at the window for a brief moment, wondering where and how the softening-up process had started inside me. Why should the transition from uniform to civilian clothes make this difference? I had had the right on my side—certainly as much as any soldier on a field of battle. Perhaps it was because subconsciously I had known and understood that a killing tonight would have solved nothing —it would certainly not have ended the matter of the murder of Major Craddock. Nor would it have answered even one of my questions about Anne.

I turned from the window, meaning to go down and try the front door. They had made their exit that way, for the door would open out on a spring latch. But unless they had had inside help it seemed unlikely that they had come in that way.

I thought it best to be cautious, going down the stairs. I didn't turn on the flashlight. There had been only the two of them in the driveway in front of General Cramer's house this afternoon, but I had no way of knowing how many had invaded River House.

I reached the ground floor without incident and then I saw something that jolted me. The door of the ladies' room across the foyer was opening and there was a light on inside.

I stood there, not quite believing that there could be anyone there. Then Anne Cramer stepped into view.

She was not frightened—keyed up a little, maybe, with all the excitement. Her care seemed to be for me.

"They're gone, Jason. I saw them from the window. They drove away. Did they hurt you?"

She was coming toward me. It was dark but not so dark that I couldn't see the outline of her. She was hatless, dressed in skirt and blouse. When she was close enough, it seemed natural that I steady her with my arm. I had the rifle in one hand and the stock struck against her thigh and I could feel the muscular reaction as she pulled a little away from it.

I said, "I forgot I was holding it," and reached over to lean the rifle down against the wall, but her arms had gone around my neck and for the moment I could not move. For the moment I did not want to move.

Her breath was quick and sweet and her hair had the scent of some tropical flower. I thought, *She worried about me—that's why she's here* . . . And then, for some moments, I thought of nothing. Her mouth had met mine in the darkness.

After a minute she took her lips away, but left her arms around my neck. She said, "I had to see you, and it was impossible to get away this afternoon or evening. I made the mistake of thinking that I could slip out of the house unnoticed after midnight. They followed me. But I fooled them. My car is over on Corset Lane. I came here on foot. They only guessed that. They came to check up—they almost trapped me. For some reason—" she giggled— "they couldn't bring themselves to look in the powder room."

"How did you get in without a key?"

"I cut the screen in your kitchen door, reached in and lifted the hook. They must have followed."

I stood there in the dark still holding her and the rifle, too. None of it was quite right in my mind. There was a pattern here, and it made sense after a fashion, but it was an unfamiliar pattern.

"Why would they care where you went?" I asked her.

"Major Craddock brought them here as bodyguards. He's had trouble—personal trouble—with some of the men on Father's project."

"Not the kind of trouble that would require bodyguards."

"No?" she said. "You didn't know Major Craddock too well. Besides, as Father's right-hand man, he controlled a substantial investment."

"You mean, somebody wanted to take that away from him?"

She said, "I don't know anything for certain." Her arms stirred about my neck. "Besides, I don't want to talk about it now. Let's just say that the major had been tough with a lot of people in his time. I think that neither he—nor the general—ever liked to be persuaded to do anything against their will."

I grinned in the darkness. "That could be."

But any amusement I felt was short-lived. We were involved in murder and a lot more questions were crowding me. I said, "Let's forget that angle for a minute. I was trying to get in touch with you. I thought of something important. It wasn't until after you had gone home this noon that I got to wondering about the D.A.'s investigator—Hoyle."

She said very quickly, "What about him?" and I guessed from her tone of voice that she, too, had recognized the danger in him.

"He was shrewd enough to come here this afternoon and check with Armando to see if I had made a night deposit after closing. That would have ruined the alibi you gave me. But Armando took credit for making the deposit. I don't think that the police, who saw me casually, could swear to the difference between us. The only one who might is a streetwalker who stopped me in front of the bank."

She said, mildly curious, "Did you go with her?"

"No. A police car came along just then. She ran down the block to River Street."

"But this wasn't the reason you were trying to get in touch with me this afternoon?" she said.

"No. I thought of something else. I heard in the bar that they had not broadcast the name of the suspect they had picked up—meaning me. How did you know they had me?"

She said, "I saw them taking you into the court house this morning when I drove past. I'd been to town to get the morning papers."

I almost laughed. It was so easy and simple. No mystic communion between us, as I had thought and been afraid to believe in. This I believed. I wondered if Hoyle would. I said, "Even so—that alibi you gave me took lots of courage."

She said, "Did it? It was the only thing that I could think of to say. And it was no near to what might have happened last night that I was hardly aware that I was lying." Her arms were suddenly tighter around my neck. "The real reason I had to come and talk to you tonight was—I got to thinking, today, about what must be going through your mind. You're not stupid. You must have realized that in alibiing you I gave myself an alibi."

I said, "But you weren't a suspect."

"Wasn't I?" she said. "Major Craddock lived at our house. He was my father's right-hand man. I don't think it's any secret that he—liked me."

"You mean he was jealous of you?" I said.

"Let's say he had a way of trying to run my life for me."

"I got that impression from some remarks he made to me. But he quoted your father."

She said, "His coming to see you was entirely his idea. My father is too busy to know or care what I do—whom I'm seen with, or where."

64

"One other thing," I said. "We used your car to tour the brickyards. Your car tracks are right there at the clay pit. And you're a big strong girl."

She said, "Hoyle will think of that angle, too, but what good will it do him? I couldn't have struck the major over the head and dumped his body into the clay pit—not when I was here at River House with you all night."

I said softly, "Where were you last night, Anne? Where were you, really?"

She said, "I was at home, asleep in my own bed, but I can't prove it. There was a party at the country club. Father insisted that I go, but I went home early. The major thought I'd come here and came to see you. He went back to the club and told Father that you had attacked him with a blackjack and that he had duly reported the fact to the police."

I said, "You left the party and went home. You went to bed and to sleep. The servants didn't hear you. The major's friends from out of town hadn't arrived yet. And when you woke up this morning you heard on the radio that the major had been killed. When you went down for the Sunday papers you saw the sheriff and the D.A.'s man and the trooper taking me in for questioning. So you fixed things for both of us."

She said, "That's my story, darling. How do you like being stuck with it? I'm bad, I guess? But I'm very good when I'm bad. You don't mind too much—tell the honest truth now, do you?"

"Mind? Me?" I had still not let her go; she seemed to have no inclination to move out of the circle of my arms. She fitted there as though that were the sole purpose and function of her being on earth. I said, "I guess you know the answer all right."

She said. "Then why don't you kiss me?"

I saw no reason not to. I couldn't see her as a murderess—

65

except, perhaps, in self-defense. There was a minute or two when it did not matter where we were, whether it was morning or night, sunshine or moonlight.

When she took her mouth away it was only to whisper against my cheek. Her whisper said, "Well, aren't you going to invite a lady up? I understand you have some good books in your library."

I said, "Sure. Sure you're invited up. But you'll be the only rare edition there."

We must have looked funny going up the stairs, our arms around each other and me still carrying the rifle. But what I was thinking was even funnier. I was wondering . . . *Were there any other car tracks at the clay pit?*

7

WHEN I went down to breakfast the next morning I went down alone. We do not serve breakfast at River House, except to the help, and I usually eat at a small table near the kitchen.

I rapped on the door between dining room and kitchen and went in. Franz was already in whites. I know that he resents the intrusion, but I fry my own eggs and ask no odds of Franz.

He was even busier than usual. I guessed some of it was put on.

I said, "Hi, Franz, what gives?"

He has a way of shrugging that might or might not be an act. I thought he gave me an odd look. I could feel tension in the room tight as drying rawhide.

"This morning, already," he said, "trouble starts."

"What is it this time?" I asked.

He turned around from the big range and gestured with the spatula in his hand. "The police," he said, "have been here again already, this morning."

This is never good news—it is especially bad before breakfast.

I said, "Hoyle?" because to me that name denoted the only police that really mattered at the moment.

"Hoyle—yes. That was the name."

"Why didn't you call me?" I wondered if I would always feel as jumpy as this, from here on.

"There was no point in calling you, Jason. It was about a young lady who might have spent last night here. I told him no young lady ever stayed here."

My stomach muscles contracted. I wondered if Hoyle had seen Anne leave. She had slipped out just before dawn.

I said, "Did he believe you?"

"I don't think so."

"Why?"

"When I came to work I saw the green Mercury parked on Corset Lane with all-night dew on its hood." Corset Lane is the local nickname for the short stretch of road connecting Brickyard Avenue with the country club road. "He may have seen it too. He did not mention it."

I forgot about the eggs. I thought coffee would be enough.

I said, "Thanks, Franz," and took the cup of coffee out to the little table near the door. The coffee was hot, but for the first time in my memory tasteless.

It took me a minute to realize that at least maybe one good thing had come out of Hoyle's early morning snooping. What he had learned, if anything, tended to support the alibi Anne had given me for the time of Craddock's murder. But why was he still snooping around?

That was a question I couldn't answer. I looked around at the familiar rooms—at River House, my house. Slowly, as if pulling out of a morass that had tangled their flow, my thoughts came into focus, shaped to a familiar design. I had work to do, here and now. Work that denied outward intrusion—that was part of the life pattern I had set myself.

To hell with Craddock, with Hoyle and his bungling investigation—to hell, almost, with Anne. And then I made a switch on the last—*God save Anne.*

I went in and sat down at the desk. I got out my records,

picked up a pencil. I thought of my mind as a slate and sponged off all marks save those pertaining to me and River House. I bent over the desk and the figures started to march. The week ahead arranged itself as it had in the past, compellingly.

It was after twelve when I came out of the office. I wondered what kind of crowd we had for lunch. It would be possible to judge that from the bar and anyway I needed a drink. But when I entered the barroom I saw that Armando's attention had been diverted. Somethink was happening outside in the parking lot.

I thought first of Hoyle, of course. I was jumpy and maybe I had a reason to be, but thinking back it seems to me that right then I was building Hoyle up too much in my mind.

I wanted that drink. I went over to see what was attracting Armando's attention had been diverted. Something was good barman that is purely a reflex action. He was not paying attention to the glass. His eyes shifted over the customers now and then, but mostly he watched the parking lot.

When I reached a position in front of him, I followed his gaze. At first I detected nothing out of the ordinary—then I saw that Eloise Ruysdale and a girl companion were getting out of her car. They were taking their time about it, curiously surveying the house and grounds.

I have wondered why it is that a man will always make it his business to watch a girl get out of a car. It may be because this is one of the most revealing actions a woman will perform—and some have perfected it to a fine art.

Both the Ruysdale girl and her companion belonged to the last category—their emergence was eminently successful. Having met Eloise, I focused my attention on her companion. I saw an attractive brunette, interestingly curved and extremely well packaged, absorbedly sizing up River House. I didn't have to guess that the splendid tan of her face and neck and bare shoulders was related to a recent sea voyage. Some waking memory told me that this might be Sue Prescott, just in from Europe, and extremely interested in what had happened to her former home. ,

Eloise came around to her side of the car and the two girls started toward the foyer to the main dining room, ignoring the bar. I decided against the drink and went to meet them, without saying anything to Armando. I was curious about Sue Prescott.

Eloise saw me, halted her companion and beckoned. "Jason," she said, "I want you to meet Sue Prescott. Sue, this is Jason Broome, who now owns River House."

I remembered the cool poise of Anne Cramer the first time I had met her and now I saw the same sort of poise in Sue Prescott. It must rub off money, I thought, and in that moment I realized how a judge at a beauty contest must feel when he has to cast the deciding vote between a long-stemmed perfect blonde and her opposite number in a darker shade.

I said, "How do you do, Miss Prescott?"

Sue Prescott's eyes were very clear, a deep, sinking brown. But there was something else about those eyes, humor and kindliness. She looked at me as if she understood me—understood both River House and me—without a word being spoken.

When she smiled, I realized she knew other things as well—she had a deep awareness of herself in relation to others. Her smile was warm, accepting a tribute she must have been used to, bestowing a tribute of her own. With Sue Prescott, I realized in that moment of our first meeting, all persons were human.

I heard Eloise say, "Sue is just in from Europe and of course she was curious to see River House."

I said, "I'll be delighted to show Miss Prescott through the house. But I'm going to have to ask something in return

—I have a table reserved in the corner of the music room. Won't you two join me for lunch?"

Sue Prescott looked at Eloise and Eloise nodded ever so slightly. When she turned back to me, her eyes were amused. Her voice came to me like a remembered echo, rich, steady and deep. I felt a little startled, as if an impossible vision of my youth had suddenly come true. I had never thought of Sue Prescott in these terms, not even when we both were young.

I should remember what that lunch conversation was about. I can't. The two of them sat across from me and talked. Europe was the conversation and so were the Americas, from here to Patagonia. Sue Prescott had traveled. My thoughts kept traveling too—from Anne to Craddock and this moment, from my first awareness of this Valley to an uncharted future.

With an effort, I stayed with the present. I made what I hoped were appropriate remarks—I tried to be a host. Presently I knew there was an interruption. I looked up, and Anne Cramer stood by our table.

She said, "Sue! Sue Prescott!" and Sue got up and they threw their arms around each other. I was a little surprised. The tall dark ones are seldom demonstrative in public. But Anne was bubbling with vitality. I could see her quivering under the white silk dress. I guessed suddenly that her regard for Sue Prescott was less than her need to express herself, less than her own abundant head of steam, requiring nervous outlet. Well, we both had something to be nervous about.

I stood with a dangling napkin in my hand. In due course Anne turned to me and her smile was bright and brittle. It never reached her eyes.

"I can forgive you now," she said, "for not waiting to have lunch with me. Sue is one of my oldest friends."

I had to go along with it. I said, "You were so late that I was sure you weren't coming."

I went around to move a chair for her while the waiter hurried in with another setting. We sat down again and once more the talk began to swirl around my head. But there was this difference. Anne's voice was directing the conversation; Anne's gestures were dominating the scene. She had taken over. I think I understood in that moment that she always would.

Sue Prescott had made a deep impression on me, but Anne's high-willed personality was taking charge of my thoughts as well. I felt relieved. I could understand how, having once loved Anne, a man would find himself forever committed. She was what I had sensed her to be from the start—the basic female, a little predatory, very sure of herself, possibly in order to hide a small, ultimate insecurity in some secret part of her.

When we had finished lunch I showed Sue Prescott through River House. Anne and Eloise came with us, of course. I had intended, without thinking too much of it at the time, to confine the tour only to the business premises. Sue Prescott had not asked to see the living quarters upstairs. But Anne took charge somewhere along the way and it was Anne who was running things at the end.

I don't think that Sue Prescott minded ending the tour. I had had a chance from time to time to see her face and some of the earlier warmth was gone from it. Plainly there were things about River House, particularly under Anne's presentation, that she either did not believe in—or could not accept.

She had once lived in this house—yet I sensed her reaction was not entirely to the destruction of familiar things, of old traditions. Anne was reminiscing all the way. "Do you remember this room, Sue? It was your mother's private sitting room, wasn't it? Remember how your father had to ask permission to enter? That seems amusing now, doesn't it? Like mustache cups. I wonder what ever became of your father's collection of those, Sue?"

At another time, she said, "And this was the playroom, Remember? We all came over one Christmas day—let's see, we were about twelve then—"

"It was snowing," Sue said. She wore a distant look. Her words had the effect of punctuation—a period.

Anne said, surprisingly, "I hate snow. I don't think I want to remember that Christmas when we were twelve. Wouldn't it be better to remember when we were twenty and it was New Year's and we were in Nassau?"

Nassau, I thought, and we were out of the woods again. I was grateful to Anne, and thought it was time for the girls to have a drink.

Eloise wanted a pink lady and this seemed right and appropriate. Sue would have a collins. I looked at Anne, for her order, and saw in her eyes what we would be having. I went to the bar and brought back the pink lady and the collins and the pair of whiskey sours. She had been drinking whiskey sours the night I first met her.

When Sue and Eloise arose to go they looked at Anne. She shook her head and said, "I'm staying a little longer— I really came to ask Jason's advice about something." She smiled at me and I smiled at her and looked at the clean fresh sweetness of her and thought how lucky I was.

But my gaze followed Sue, briefly, as she followed Eloise to their car and there was something about the tilt of her head and the straight even stride of her that bothered me.

As Anne and I turned toward the barroom, she said, "That was an ordeal, Jason. After all, I almost grew up here too and seeing her brought back so many memories." Her small, perfect teeth showed briefly, sank gently into her full lower lip, her blue eyes looked hurt.

I said, "Let's take another table—just for us—and let me

bring you a drink."

She said, "I shouldn't be here. The major's funeral is tomorrow. There are all sorts of things to attend to—besides appearances."

I tried to imagine her as a slave to appearances. The picture refused to materialize. We went to a corner table and I told Armando to bring two more whiskey sours. When he came, with his little tray, he leaned toward me.

"That county detective is back—that guy Hoyle. I just seen him parking out in the lot."

"So?"

Armando gave a shrug. He said, "Boss, I hope he can't find jam on your face under a microscope. You know what he strikes me as? He strikes me as a guy who ain't ever going to give up."

I said, "Just call him nemesis," and glanced at Anne.

She evinced no concern. She had wedged herself into the corner. We smiled and toasted each other, and I turned to watch the door. I wanted to see him as he came through my door.

This time he bothered with no one else, but came straight to our table. He looked purposive, though not impressive. I did not stand up and hoped by not doing so to embarrass him and make him feel unwelcome. I was afraid of Hoyle and my fear was beginning to show in rudeness.

He was not a very dapper figure of a man. His summer suit was wrinkled and there was a small gravy stain on the leg of his trousers. He pulled a chair over and sat down.

"This is official," he said. He said it quietly. Then he stared at us a moment, spilling cigar ash on a knit necktie that didn't go with a summer suit. He brushed the ash away and the gesture was as tired as his eyes.

"Miss Cramer," he said at last, "I don't like to come barging in on your social life, but you know how these things are. A man gets murdered—we just can't leave it that

74

way. Do you want to tell me anything you know or can remember about a man named Howard Carter?"

I glanced at Anne and was startled. There was a dumb blonde sitting next to me—if you ever saw a dumb blonde. How do they do that routine? The mouth is just a little open, moist and faintly pouting. The eyes aren't quite blank; there is a hint of a bewildered smile in the depths of them. The golden hair shines and the skin is fresh and lovely and the hands reach out and toy with a cigarette or an ashtray or a whiskey sour.

"Howard Carter?" she said, and even her voice was empty. "Now let me see." You would have sworn that she was trying to think and could find nothing at all to use for the job, inside that small and lovely skull.

I don't know whether Hoyle was enjoying it or not, but I think he appreciated the situation. A slow flush started somewhere under his tired expression, rose to the surface, and suddenly he looked both formidable and angry.

"Well?" he said, ignoring me and giving his full attention to Anne, "What about it? Can you help me out?"

"Carter?" she said. "Howard Carter?"

I thought that she was beginning to brighten. A lot of tension, I sensed, had gone out of her. Her foot found mine under the table—its pressure was steady, constant.

Hoyle said, leaning forward. "That's the name. Has he been in town lately? Was he up to see your father—the general, that is?"

"I knew a Howard Carter," Anne said. "When my father and the major were building a big housing project in the Midwest a couple of years ago, he worked for them."

Hoyle said, "I'm not interested in that. I work for the district attorney's office—county government. What I want to know is, has Carter been in town within the past week? Is he the same Carter who got into a fight with the major in Chicago and was beaten up by the major and some of his friends?"

"How did you learn about that?" Anne asked.

Hoyle sighed and relit his cigar. "Oh, I'm a great brain," he said. "A sort of super-detective. I find these things out. This tip came anonymously from a pay booth at the edge of town in a gas station where the attendant can't remember what the caller looked like. 'Just check up,' says a voice on the phone, 'and see if Howard Carter was in town the night Major Craddock was murdered. Craddock almost killed him in Chicago.' That's all I know. So I'm asking."

She said, "I didn't make any such phone call, if that's what you're thinking."

"It was a man's voice," Hoyle said wearily.

"Oh. Well, all right then. There was a Howard Carter. The major did have a fight with him. In fact Major Craddock was arrested, but the charges were dropped. Does that help?"

"Not much. You haven't told us anything that we haven't already found out from the Chicago police. But maybe you could tell us something that they can't. Was Carter in town the night the major was killed?"

I found myself holding my breath.

Anne looked straight at Hoyle and said, "How would I know? I certainly didn't see him."

He might have trapped her then and there, if she had said, "Yes," or even, "Maybe." Now a grudging sort of appreciation showed in his eyes.

He said, "Miss Cramer, your boy friend here is still being investigated. If you could have placed this Howard Carter in town looking for Craddock last Saturday night the police would not have had to bother you again. As it happens, I doubt you could have made it stick."

He got up while he was talking. He shoved his chair

against the table, hiking the tablecloth up, nodded and walked away.

She turned to me and said, "What do you make of that? *You're* still under suspicion."

I kicked Hoyle's chair out a little so that the tablecloth dropped back into place. I squeezed her hand and tried to grin. "Let's make nothing of it—for now."

8

WHEN Hoyle was gone, curious glances were thrown our way. I said to Anne, "Let's get out of here." The air-conditioning at River House was the best available, but in spite of all I'd spent on it, it wasn't getting fresh air to me fast enough. I needed room to breathe—away from people.

"My car is just outside the door," she said. "We can take that."

I had been thinking about her car, and the tire marks at the brickyard. I said, "Maybe we'd better take my car this time, especially if you want to drive down to the pit. My car has been checked. My tires don't match the cast the police made of tire marks already there."

We were outside, walking swiftly, but she had turned toward her green Mercury. She smiled at me over her shoulder.

"So you've been worrying about that," she said. "I realized when I heard where they had found the body that they might check my car. After all, I have thrust myself into the case pretty spectacularly. If they found my tire marks on the scene, it could be embarrassing."

I knew almost without asking. I said, "You're riding on new tires?"

She got under the wheel herself this time. She smiled and said, "It wasn't easy to arrange without arousing suspicion, but it was the reason I left you so quickly yesterday at the court house. I'm curious—how would you have gone about it, Jason?"

She opened her car door, got in. I got in beside her. For some reason I knew a sense of great relief. But she had asked me a question and I hadn't answered. I said, "You ran over some glass and ruined all four tires. So you bought four new ones—"

She said, "Jason, you would be in trouble. Four ruined tires—any garageman would remember that and talk about it. I had my tires changed one at a time in four different places. It cost me the price of four rusty nails plus the price of the tires in four different parts of the township. Each time I had a flat near a gas station, but far enough for me to ruin the tire getting there. Now I really would like to see the brickyard again."

I said, "Your old tires—where are they?"

She laughed. She said, "One of them is at the city dump and who can say how it got there? Another is in a ditch in the high weeds out on the ridge road. A third is in Cedar Pond and the fourth one rolled across the state road and buried itself under the leaves in Clancy's woods."

I said, "But if someone saw you—"

"No one saw me."

I said soberly, "That was a lot of trouble to go to. We could have safely admitted that we were at the brickyard in your car. We had a right to be there."

She said, "Of course. Would you also like to try to prove to the jury that either one of us—or any decent citizen—had a perfect right to kill Major Craddock?"

I said the only thing. "Meaning exactly what?"

"Not what you think. I'm not confessing to murder for either of us. I'm only pointing out that someone might have

79

taken my car during the night and moved the body to the clay pit in it."

"Someone?" I said. "What are you trying to tell me?"

"Nothing—yet. I really have nothing to go on. And if I ever do—I'm not sure I'll go to the police with it."

I felt a little shocked. What she hinted was that someone might have taken her car to move Craddock's body from her house to the clay pit—some other resident of the Cramer mansion than herself.

A servant? I didn't think she meant the servants. One of the major's stooges? That could be, but why would she be reluctant then to go to the police? That left the general himself—her father, General Gunther Cramer. Was she trying to imply that she suspected her father of having killed Craddock?

I couldn't accept that—not just yet.

I asked, "Anne, about this Howard Carter. Did Hoyle have something in his anonymous phone tip? Did you tell Hoyle all you know?"

She nodded. "As much as I know. The major and some of his goons gave Carter a beating a couple of months ago for some reason I'm not clear on. But Carter was never in town. I'm sure of that. He would have been out to the house trying to patch things up. He had a real money-making proposition, if he could have sold the general on it."

"If he had come to kill the major, wouldn't he have shown up at the house?"

"I'm trying to tell you—Carter wasn't the type."

I said, "There is no such thing as the killer type. That's hogdip. Any man will kill under the proper circumstances— I mean with enough provocation or a good enough motive. Did Craddock oppose his selling his proposition to your father?"

"I don't think so. Even if he had, Carter was full of ideas

for making easy money. Too full of such ideas to go around killing anyone."

"Then what are you implying—that your father killed Craddock?"

She stopped the car. For a moment she rested her blonde head on her arms, against the wheel, and her head was lovely.

"I don't know," she said at last, huskily. "That's the hell of it—I don't know. I only know that you didn't do it and that I had to protect both of us somehow. But I can't help him—I never could."

I thought of the general as I had seen him. A tall, heavy man with gray hair, a brush mustache and eyebrows almost as thick as the mustache. He walked solidly, with authority, and was said to be a brilliant, ruthless, driving sort of a man. Capable of murder? Certainly—but, not the likeliest suspect. I doubted the police had ever considered him.

The cigar had gone to dead ash that spilled on my shirt. I threw it away and blew down at the ash. I tried to think clearly. I was sure of one thing only—I had not killed Craddock. Who had? Anne—the general? Or, and here I hoped fervently, a person unknown?

Anne raised her head and leaned toward me. I put my arm around her.

"Since you considered it first," I said, "let's consider it some more. Let's try to chase this nightmare. Why would the general have killed Craddock? They were friends as well as business associates."

She bit her lower lip. The act made her look very young and defenseless. Her voice, when she spoke, was barely audible.

"It could have been because of me."

"You?"

"Craddock was—well, it isn't easy to say. He was possessive. He interfered a great deal in everything I did—"she threw me a sidelong glance—"like my coming to River House."

I said, "I've wanted to hear about that—from you, I mean."

She looked straight at me. She said, "I was at River House for lunch on Saturday. Remember?"

"Of course."

"You invited me back for the evening."

"That's right."

"I intended to come back. I went home and started to get ready. I was alone in the house except for the maid. I took a bath—and was coming down the hall to my room when the major walked in. I was wearing slippers and a terry robe and that's all."

I looked at her. I didn't say anything. I waited.

"He and the general had been at the construction office that afternoon. Craddock came home early. Somewhere, somehow, from someone, he had heard about my being at River House, that I had been driving with you. I suppose he guessed you and I had another date. It annoyed him and we argued. The major was the kind of a man who can lay his hands on a woman when he's arguing."

I said, "Your father came home and saw you arguing?"

She said wryly, "It was almost a wrestling match by that time. And remember how I was dressed."

I said, "Your idea is that he brooded about his daughter's honor—and that night he killed Craddock?"

She was annoyed. She said, with an odd inflection, "*You* might take a thing like that lightly."

"I'm not taking it lightly. It's a good motive for murder. One of the best. It just seems a little odd to me that you suggested it."

There was no anger in her eyes now. They were completely calm, entirely reasonable. "Can't you understand that sooner or later someone else is going to propose him as a suspect?"

I considered that. I wanted to ask who, but sensed that this was not the time.

Instead I said, "You went to the country club that night instead of coming to River House. Was it because your father insisted that you go—or because the major wanted you there?"

"That's right. Craddock had an explanation of our tussle in the hall—you were the reason. Craddock explained that I had been going to River House and planned to return there Saturday night. So father said that I was to go to the club—it was an order."

I thought about that. Finally I said, "If your father killed Craddock to protect your honor—you sort of booted his defense around when you told the D.A. that you had spent all night Saturday night with me."

I expected her to take a swing at me. I wouldn't have minded—it would have been an honest, healthy reaction. We had both been getting morbid without making any progress, and I wanted to snap us out of it.

"I guess I asked for that," she said. One corner of her mouth twisted. "Perhaps we've said enough—and now that we have, what do you want to do?"

She sat there beside me in that sleek summer dress and asked me that. I thought she looked even lovelier in that moment than she had when I first met her, for by now we had mutual experiences to share. I suppose I had an impulse to make love to her, but I sensed—and I think she felt it, too—that this once more was not the time, or the place.

We sat in silence for some moments. At last she shrugged. "I think we ought to go back. I've got to see my father—and there are arrangements to be made for tomorrow."

I said nothing. She spun the wheel over and we started

back up the hill. The brickyards and the clay pit were left to their lazy day in the sun.

We had nothing to say to each other on the way back. She pulled up in front of the gateposts of River House and I got out. I stood for a few seconds leaning on the door of the car and looking at her.

She said, "You won't be there tomorrow, will you?" and I understood her to refer to the funeral. I said that I wouldn't.

She said, "Of course the police sometimes come, hoping that something significant will happen."

I knew that by "police" she meant Hoyle. I supposed, too, that Hoyle would be there. Hoyle was a man to see his duty and do it.

I said, "I am afraid that nothing significant will happen."

She had no answer. She gave me a brief wave and drove away. I turned and walked up the bluestone drive to River House. I felt a great weariness, the sort of old-age ache that should not be in my bones for another thirty years. I was too tired to reason—but I remember a brief, blind moment during that walk when, thinking of Anne and of what we had said and been to each other, I almost wished I had killed Major Craddock.

I went directly to the bar. Armando saw me coming and my drink was ready when I reached for it. He said, "There were no police here while you were gone," and I could not tell from his blank expression whether this was meant as humor or as a simple statement of fact.

I sat at the bar for awhile, hunched forward, sipping my drink and understanding better than ever before why bars do business.

Armando let the ever-widening circle of the bar cloth come closer to my elbow. "Do you think it's a good thing that Hoyle is taking his business somewhere else?"

I said that I didn't know. I said, "It's hard to tell what's in his mind. Maybe he's realized by now that Anne and I are really in the clear."

"I hope so," Armando said. "I was wondering just now if he might be checking on the goon squad—the strong-arm boys out of the major's past."

"Army buddies." I dismissed the idea.

"Look," Armando said, "no two enlisted men were ever buddies of a major. You know that."

I said, "The army took all kinds. They couldn't keep all the riffraff out. Besides, the major's boys would have an alibi."

"Who hasn't?" Armando said and it was hardly a question.

I thought I'd try it on him for size. I said, "I heard the general hasn't."

Armando didn't finish the circle he was working on. The bar cloth came to a moist and sodden halt. He bent toward me, his head tipped up and his gaze was suddenly sharp and questioning.

"This is a new angle," he said.

I held up a clenched fist. I opened the thumb. "Not me," I said. I raised the index finger. "Not Anne." With the second finger I said, "Not you, certainly!" Then I lifted the last two, "If not the goons from the major's past, who is left except the general?"

He said, "If you're asking me, I'd say nuts to that. The major was the drive behind all the general's plans. He was the whip. Without him, they tell me, the general has trouble. Besides, they were friends. Skip the general, that's my reaction."

"I kind of thought so, too. But friends fall out over the damnedest things, I've heard." I shook my head at him. "That's all, Armando."

He looked at me worriedly for seconds, then moved down the bar.

The place was beginning to fill up now with some of the after-lunch golfers from the club. I thought Armando could handle them—and suddenly I had a great need to be alone. I caught his eye, waved to him and went back out to the parking lot and got into my own car.

I didn't know just where I was going, but I had always liked to drive. I didn't want to talk or think, and yet I had the feeling of having to keep in motion. Something was nagging at the back of my mind—nothing very important, I suspected, but insistent nevertheless. If I could be alone, my hands and feet occupied with driving, my thoughts and attention on the traffic, something might happen to release my mental bottleneck.

Nothing much did. Still, I learned something that dissolved the knot at the back of my brain and gave me a new slant on the problem facing Anne and myself.

I drove out into the country, not too far out, but skirting the town on familiar, less traveled roads. Gradually the feel of the wheel under my hands, the sound of the tires, the lift and fall of the country around me, of the road under me, began to work its usual magic. I found my spirits rising —and my foot sinking on the accelerator.

The speedometer picked up to sixty, seventy. I knew the exhilaration of speed, of freedom, of flight from the past morbid hours—the horses under my hood were nothing special, yet they were adequate and responsive. I kept my eye on the rear-view mirror and my thoughts on Anne—but only on her loveliness.

I did not think of her as a possible killer.

I saw the gray car take shape in the mirror, and my foot eased automatically on the gas pedal. The state police car was close; he must have clocked me, and I braced myself for a ticket or a lecture. Such was my feeling of release, however, that I wouldn't have minded either—when suddenly the gray car swerved off the road, pulling into a gas station I had just passed.

At first the significance of this fact didn't register. I drove on, more slowly now, congratulating myself on a narrow escape. Lucky the trooper had just then run out of gas, I thought—when suddenly the nagging knot in my mind dissolved and I remembered the tire tracks at the pit and Anne's story about changing the Mercury's rubber.

I made a U-turn and drove back slowly. As I passed the gas station, I saw the trooper talking to the attendant. His notebook was out and he was busy with his jottings. The gray car was parked to one side, not near the gas pumps.

And so my ephemeral lift of spirits was gone—I was back in my world of murder and suspicion and violence. I drove slowly now, and with a purpose. I checked enough gas stations to be sure—at some of them I was known. Anne's account of how she had managed to get new tires on the green Mercury had seemed clever enough at the time she told it—but it hadn't fooled Hoyle and it hadn't fooled the troopers. Every gas station and every tire dealer in town was being checked for recent tire purchases, and the troopers were taking down descriptions of each purchaser.

I thought of Anne's loveliness—they would remember her. I thought of the alibi we shared, which suddenly seemed a brittle thing, fragile and breakable, for all that it involved her honor.

I drove back to River House, parked on the blue gravel, went in through the bar and Armando said, "Did the drive do you any good, boss?"

I said, "It's funny you should have asked that," and went on to my office and sat down at my desk. I reached out for the telephone but I didn't pick it up. I shifted my hand over to the cigar humidor instead. I took a long time trimming and lighting the cigar.

MURDER WITHOUT TEARS

I wondered what in the hell to do now. Anne would be at the funeral parlor tonight, and I didn't dare call her at her home. There would be extensions at the Cramer mansion and anyone might listen in. I suddenly had the sense that we were not sharing an alibi—Anne and I—but were caught in a shared trap.

The walls of the small office began closing in on me, and I went back to the bar. Armando waited for the nod, caught it and brought me a drink. A man and a girl sat at the end of the bar and only a few couples were scattered around the room. It was the early dinner hour—too soon for the crowd to arrive. Still the place was emptier than usual.

"Thin tonight," Armando said.

"It's early still," I said. "Besides, a lot of our regulars will be attending Major Craddock tonight."

It was strange to think of murder affecting business at the River House.

"Will they have MP's in uniform there?" Armando asked wryly.

I didn't think it was anything to joke about. I said, "Skip the wisecracks, Armando. Tell me—Hoyle hasn't been back? Or the state police?"

"Nobody," Armando said. "We're being slighted. Why don't you go down to the funeral parlor and see what gives? Things will be dead around here tonight—Monday night blues."

I said, "I don't want any part of it." I had another drink. It was time I walked away from the bar—I had been drinking most of the day. But this time I didn't feel like walking away—instead I studied my glass. It held a subtle magic. I liked the color of the drink, the way the light struck through the dark glass opalescence and played across the ripples when I moved it.

I emptied the glass and half expected Armando's eye-

88

brows to rise as I shoved the glass toward him. But his face was as expressionless as a griddlecake.

I said, "Okay. It might come to that some day. It hasn't come to that yet." I waited for Armando to say something in reply. He didn't say anything.

I said, "Well?"

He said, "Maybe you're expecting applause or something?"

I said, "Armando, some day I'm going to fire you."

He said, "Some day I'm going to quit."

I cocked a fist at him and felt a little foolish and grinned. I walked out into the evening air. The sun was just behind the hills west of the town. There was a lingering glow on the river. I walked over across the road and looked at the shadow of the hill on the water.

I suppose people had stood here with problems more important than mine. At the moment my problems did not seem especially important—Craddock, I thought, was surely in a worse spot than I, facing St. Peter.

My thoughts were rather muddled—Anne, Hoyle, Craddock and his goons, the general, Sue, my youth down on the flats—a name, Howard Carter. For some reason, Carter bothered me that night. Probably because he was just a name, not a person, not even a memory, and I had some difficulty believing in him. Hell, the man probably didn't even exist.

Yet it was the anonymous tip about Howard Carter that sent Hoyle all the way to the West Coast.

And if Hoyle hadn't gone to the Coast this whole affair might have had a different ending.

9

I DROVE to town on business the next morning. I hadn't intended to watch Major Craddock's funeral cortege pass through Main Street, but my timing was poor. I saw Anne and the general in the leading limousine, but failed to find Hoyle.

I finished my business for the River House and started back along Main Street. I intended to stop for a box of cigars and the morning paper, and had just pulled to the curb when a cab cut in front of me and parked. Eloise Ruysdale waved at me from the back seat.

I went over and said good morning.

Eloise said, "I recognized your car and wondered if I could beg a lift. Did you see the show just now?"

I said, "If you mean the funeral procession, yes. And I'd be delighted to drop you anywhere you like."

"I've wanted to talk to you," she said. She fumbled in her purse and settled with the driver, while I collected the packages beside her on the car seat. We went back to my car.

As I pulled out from the curb, she said, "Jason, have you had any trouble since Major Craddock's death?"

"Nothing but," I said. "I had an argument with him the night he was killed and the police had me in for questioning."

"I heard about that," she said. "It wasn't what I meant —I was wondering if anything else had happened."

I glanced at her. She sat very erect, staring straight ahead, her hands quiet in her lap. She seemed sure of herself, not nervous, but there was tension in her posture, and an intense concentration in her profile.

"What would that mean?" I asked.

"Have you received any threats?"

I thought of the major's goon boys and their visit to River House, but since I had not reported the incident to the police I didn't want to discuss it.

I said, "Not exactly. Have you?"

She turned to me earnestly. "I don't know what to make of them—that's why I asked for this lift. I want you to come to the house and see for yourself. And talk to Sue—she's staying with me, you know."

I said, "All right," and we rode in silence, except for her directions.

We began to pass the first big estates on the outskirts of town. I though a little ironically that murder was buying me a pass into circles I could never have crashed on my own. The girl beside me, the girl waiting for us, had been beyond my pale for as long as I could remember.

The Ruysdale place was near the country club, only a short distance from where Anne lived. Generations had gone to the shaping of its grounds, and the winding driveway was flanked by what looked to be century-old trees.

When we reached the big house, Eloise said, "Drive on around to the back."

I followed the curve of the drive to what had been originally the stableyard. Now it was blacktopped, and the old carriage house had been converted to a garage. Two cars were visible beyond the open doors—one I recognized as the car I had seen Eloise driving when she and Sue had visited River House. Even from a distance I could see that something had happened to it.

I got out and went into the carriage house. The car's convertible top had been slashed to ribbons. The upholstery —a special job—had been cut, and someone had splashed red paint over the wheel, the steering post, the instrument panel, the windshield and part of the hood.

I said, "I see it—but I can hardly believe it. The kids in these parts just aren't that wild."

"That's just about the way I felt at first," Eloise said. "But a note came with the treatment. It was left in the car. It was not addressed to anyone in particular and, of course, it was unsigned. It said, 'Arizona has a very healthy climate. Much better than the Hudson Valley.' Doesn't that sound like a threat?"

I said, "When you were at River House, I seem to remember you and Miss Prescott planning a trip to Arizona."

"Yes. But later, Sue changed her mind. I think whoever wrote the note wants us to go. I can't imagine any other explanation."

"Have you discussed your change of plans with anyone?"

She shook her head. "Not with anyone in particular— except members of the family. Of course, that means that almost anyone in town might have gotten to know. Besides, nothing's settled yet. Mostly we've argued about it—I want to go."

"Have you reported this vandalism to the police?"

She nodded again. "Yes, they had no explanation. They felt that whoever was responsible must have been motivated by personal reasons. But neither Sue nor I have enemies in town. Neither of us know anyone capable of this kind of vindictiveness."

That I could believe. I came to the next point, somehow to me vitally important. "Why did Sue Prescott change her mind about leaving?"

Eloise looked at me candidly. "I'm not sure, but I've made a guess. That's why I wanted you to talk to her."

I thought that one over carefully. Eloise's open features gave me no clue. Then I remembered Sue Prescott's look during her tour of River House and had an idea.

What I felt first was a slow burn of anger. Eloise must have seen it on my face, for something like compassion seeped into her clear brown eyes.

I asked, "Has her decision to stay anything to do with River House?"

Eloise looked troubled. "I'd rather not discuss it."

I said, "If she has any idea of staying in order to persuade me to sell River House back to her, she's wasting her time." I swept my hand toward the mutilated car. "If I'm supposed to be blamed for this—let me assure you that I don't give a damn whether she stays or goes."

Eloise said sharply, "Nobody's blaming you" —then her look softened a little. "I'm sorry, Jason. I know what River House must mean to you. It doesn't mean that much to Sue, or she would have been back sooner. I wanted you to tell her that."

"In order to persuade her to leave?"

She nodded mutely.

Some of my anger was vanishing. Ordinarily I wouldn't even have flared up like that, but I was jumpy about Anne's and my position in the Craddock murder—the thing was getting to me.

I smiled, and a fleeting acknowledgement crossed Eloise's features.

"I'm sorry too," I offered. "Is Sue in the house?"

"She was asleep when I left." As we started walking toward the main house, Eloise threw a sidelong glance at me. "Please don't be harsh with her, Jason."

"I won't." This time I grinned. There was something wholesome and understanding about this girl beside me, and wholesomeness and understanding were what I needed just then. I wondered why I couldn't be sensible and fall in love with someone like her—until Anne came along, I had always preferred brunettes.

We walked along the drive to the house. The grounds about us were quiet and exuded stately antiquity. There had been a good way of life here once, I thought—perhaps some of it lingered still.

Presently I asked, "When you reported this vandalism to the state police, did they tie it up with Major Craddock's murder?"

Eloise hesitated. Her steps slowed, delaying our reaching the house. Finally she said, "No. That was my idea."

"Any good reasons?" I asked.

"None I could discuss. It's just that—that Major Craddock met death by violence and this is another instance of violence. And the note would seem to suggest something more than random vandalism."

"But the police didn't think so?"

She shook her head. "No—they thought we had picked up some unpleasant friends." She shivered. "Whoever they are, I'm ready to leave town. And if you can persuade Sue that River House is not on the market for purposes of restoration, I think she'll go with me."

We reached the house, and Sue met us in the hall, wearing a blue-and-white playsuit and sandals. She smiled at us both, but I caught an underlying soberness in her eyes when she looked at me.

Eloise wasted no time in preambles. "I've brought Jason over to discuss your problem," she said.

Sue Prescott frowned, looking from one of us to the other. "I'm afraid I don't understand."

I said, "Eloise tells me you've changed your mind about going to Arizona."

Sue stiffened, and Eloise said quickly, "In spite of the excitement last night."

There was a moment's silence. Eloise and I waited. I looked at Sue, and she looked as good to me as she had at River House. There was the same honest depth to her gaze as it met mine, but now there was a barrier between us too. Where before I had read interest and polite acquiescence, I now sensed a guarded hostility.

"Of course," Sue said. "What could last night possibly have to do with my plans? Simple vandalism."

I said, "I'm not so sure," and felt a warmth on my face at the sudden mockery in Sue's eyes.

She said very quietly, "You would like to have me leave Newburyport, wouldn't you, Mr. Broome?"

"Jason," I said. "I believe I already expressed myself on that question to Eloise." I felt the slow anger rising in myself again.

Eloise put in, "He said he didn't give a damn whether you stayed or left."

Sudden color heightened the tan on Sue's cheeks. Her voice was still quiet. "Perhaps neither of you quite understands. I intend to buy River House back." She looked directly at me, and the barrier between us was a solid, tangible thing. "I have quite a bit of money, Mr. Broome. My parents left it to me—exactly as they left you your name."

I felt my temper rising to match hers. "River House," I said, "is not for sale—at any price."

For the first time the anger reached her eyes, and something electric leaped between us. I remember thinking her magnificent in that moment—and hating her with all the roots of my being.

She said, "Perhaps not for money. But I still have influential friends. And from what I've heard, you're not entirely free of trouble."

I stared at her. I couldn't believe she meant it. I couldn't believe she actually meant to take advantage of the situation I found myself in—with Anne.

Lovely, golden Anne. I stared at Sue, and her face and Anne's seemed to merge, to become one mocking mask, an image of all I had wanted and envied others for possessing since the earliest years of my being down in the flats, the brickyards.

Not Anne, I thought—I already possessed Anne. She had sworn away her honor to defend me—she had been mine for at least one night . . . Slowly the faces drew apart, took on their separate entities. Anne's blonde and bold and giving —Sue's dark and demanding. And yet the spark was there, the attraction of two opposite poles.

I smiled at Sue Prescott. "If it comes to that, you may not find me entirely lacking in friends, Miss Prescott."

She said, "Such as broke into our garage last night?"

I said it mostly to impress her—it was foolish, I know. I said, "Perhaps even those."

I turned and strode out of that house. It did not come to me until later that, even with murder as my passport, I had not gotten beyond the front hall of that mansion.

10

THE door of my room was open. Anne's voice said, "Come in and close it, Jason."

I stepped into the room and closed the door. The air was acrid with cigarette smoke. Anne was sitting on the bed. She was fully dressed and not in mourning—she wore a print dress with a peasant blouse effect, and a skirt that did full justice to the wonderful body it sheathed.

She had an ashtray in her lap and a cigarette between two crimson-tipped fingers. Her lips curved as she said, "I'll bet you hate women who smoke in bed."

I didn't answer that. I stood there, wondering if she'd gotten drunk so early in the day. and so soon after the funeral of a man who had been her father's friend. She gave me the unwinking cat business with the eyes.

"Aren't you going to ask me about the funeral?" she said.

What was there to ask? I said, "I trust they covered up the major properly."

She giggled. "I saw to that." She patted the bed beside her. "Sit down, Jason, and listen to me for a minute."

I went over and sat down. I could smell the liquor on her breath now, and then I thought, *If anyone ever had a reason to take a few drinks, she does* . . . I felt as though I could have used a couple of Armando's specials myself.

"There," she said. "Isn't that better? Now—light a cigar."

I said, "A cigar?" and she nodded solemnly.

"We're about to hold a business conference."

"I can do business without a cigar," I said. I wanted to tell her about the state police checking on her newly-bought tires, but doubted she could properly absorb such information now.

She laughed, that husky, yielding sort of laugh. She said, "My father wants you to come to work for him."

That was a shocker.

I said, "I don't believe I know what you're talking about."

"You will," she said. "Would it make you feel more comfortable if I got up off this bed and sat at the desk— you know, formal and business-like and no nonsense?"

I said, "I guess it doesn't matter where you sit. You spoke about the general and a proposition. There must be some simple, easy way to put it."

"There is," she said. She took the time to light another cigarette. She said, "The general thinks pretty well of you —on my recommendation."

"That isn't the impression Craddock tried to give me."

"Can't we forget Craddock? Today he belongs to the ages."

I wasn't at all sure that he did, but I said, "All right, so we'll forget Craddock. Where does that leave us?"

"It leaves us standing face to face with the general's proposition again."

"You've mentioned it," I admitted. "What's its nature?"

"It's pretty simple. The general is ready to offer you Craddock's job."

I said, "Are you kidding?"

"Hardly. This is business, Jason. My father and I never kid about business. There's an opening for a good man. You're a good man."

"Am I? I'm a good man for the business I'm in. I've made a go of it. But am I any good for anything else? By the way—what *was* Craddock's job? How do you and your father define it?"

"He was the general's assistant, a liaison man. A trouble-shooter. A Washington contact. An expediter of materials. And once in a while a strong-arm boy."

I looked at her sitting on my bed, smoking my cigarettes and not as drunk as I had thought at first—in fact, now she was all business. And she might be offering me a better out from being suspected of murder than her original alibi. The general wielded a lot of power in the state—in fact, throughout the nation, and his offering me the position of his right-hand man ought even to quiet Hoyle's suspicions. I still thought of Hoyle as my main nemesis—or ours, Anne's and mine.

Still, I couldn't quite see it. I said, "If Craddock was all the things you say, he is going to be a hard man to replace. I'm not sure that I could do any one of his many jobs well —certainly I couldn't do all of them well. And one other thing—I like the life I lead. I belong where I am, doing what I do for a living."

She said, "You run a ginmill. It's a high-priced, swanky sort of a joint, but it is still a ginmill."

I said, "Some pretty important people like the way I run it."

"I know they do. But I think you've already had all the future there is in running a roadhouse in Newburyport. Father's game is much bigger. He has housing developments scattered all over the country. She swung her legs up in the air and swiveled around to a sitting position beside me. She put her arm around me, leaned her head on my shoulder and said, "We would have the world to-gether, Jason—travel, resorts—Florida in the winter, the

99

lake resorts in the summer, perhaps California in the fall—"

I said, "Craddock didn't take much of a trip—you were with him this morning."

"Don't be silly." She rubbed her cheek against my shoulder.

I didn't mind her arm around me or her head on my shoulder, but I couldn't see where I belonged in the general's big dream. I said, "Look, Anne—I haven't got it. Not what it takes for what you want. And I don't even care. Maybe what you and the general want isn't what I want —I've been happy at River House, after my fashion."

She got up, walked to the window and stood looking down at the brickyard flats. She had a stiff, hard smile on her face, the kind of smile women fight with.

"You only think you've got what you want," she said. Her voice grew gently mocking. "Little Jason Broome— working down there with the sweat in his eyes, burning brick under the summer sun. Little Jason Broome looking up at the big house and swearing some day to live up there—" she whirled away from the window and her voice was no longer gentle—"and what have you settled for? A ginmill! You couldn't make the grade any other way. You couldn't start a brickyard, or deal in stocks and bonds. You had to get here in a manner befitting your start in life. These were good homes, here on the hill—and you set a ginmill down in the midst of them."

I said, "Try to be reasonable. I bought this place after it had become a ginmill. And if I'm lowering the tone of the neighborhood, I'm sorry—but a lot of people seem to think I have a decent place. Anyway, it's more than a gin-mill. You know that. It's one of the best restaurants around these parts."

She came over to me. She put her hands on my shoulders. She seemed to move nearer to me as though through a mist. I could feel my heart pumping away, harder and harder, and there was the beginning of pressure at my temples.

"I'm sorry," she said huskily. "I'm sorry, Jason. I wasn't belittling you. But you don't know your own potential. You'll settle for little things, Jason, when there are big things to be had."

I was trying to find some kind of words to tell her that maybe the little things were all that I wanted, that the price of the big things came too high. Craddock, for one, had paid the price, though I didn't know how or why. And because I didn't know, it would all have sounded a little silly just then. I decided not to say anything.

She was pressing against me now—I could smell her perfume and suddenly it was not a business conference any longer . . .

She pushed away from me after a minute and said, "Jason!" and looked at me reproachfully. "I didn't have anything like that in mind. Today is only for business." She did deft things with her hair and shrugged her dress into place. She said, "I really have to be going, but I want to tell my father that you're in favor of working for him and that we can set up a meeting to brief you on your duties. Of course you'll have to get rid of this place."

I got up. I said, "Or get someone to run it for me." I was still cautious, still unsure, but somehow her idea had begun to take hold. "Wait, Anne—"

"Yes, Jason?" She had moved to the door. She waited, pleasantly, the warm, half smile on her face.

I said, "There's one part of our being together we haven't discussed. If I'm to work for your father—if we're to be together—" I hesitated, not knowing quite how to put it, or even what I wanted to say.

She said it for me, smiling. "Oh, father won't insist on

marriage. He's always had a dream about my being married to someone influential—someone who could really help him, perhaps a U. S. Senator—"

She left it on an unfinished note. I sat and stared.

She was laughing and, laughing, she went out the door.

11

NIGHT is not a good time anywhere, except for lovers. It is never a good time for a man alone. This night I felt more alone than ever before.

I drowsed and awoke restlessly to the slightest sound, whether that of a passing car or some noise in the garden behind the house. For the first time since River House had become my sole interest, I was not fretting over the day's take. My thoughts revolved around two points—Anne's laughing exit this afternoon, and my earlier quarrel with Sue. Partly, too, I was alert against a return visit by the friends of Major Craddock. It was not until the small hours that sleep took me solidly, and even then I saw in swirling, misted dreams a road underwater, a clay cart fathoms down, and finally a bottomless clay pit with all the dark and gruesome fascination of a still pool of black water mirroring the cold vigilance of the stars.

These were not good things to dream—but reality, when I awoke to it, was even worse.

I awoke to the crash of glass and window frames and a shuddering and a shaking of the house itself, as though some geologic fault had set off another of the valley's occasional mild earthquakes. I awoke, reaching for the gun that was always near the bed now, and always loaded. I jumped into loafers, yanked a pair of trousers over my pajamas and went down the stairs with a rush.

Glass was smashing all around me. Bottles behind the bar, the bar mirror itself, glass in the doors between bar and foyer; front-door glass, window glass—anything fragile was coming apart in shards and fragments. Going down the second flight of stairs I heard an axe bite into wood, and felt the stairs tremble.

In the corridor, racing along the second floor, I heard pans and kettles go in the kitchen. Cupboards of chinaware were wrenched and torn from the walls. A man-made devastation, as unbelievable as a bomb in church, was ruining the lower floor of River House.

I had thought, of course, of the two friends of Major Craddock, the ex-MP's. When I reached the ground floor I was carrying the light rifle at the ready, and I did not have to see the devastation to know that I was going to do my best to kill someone this time—if I could find someone to kill.

As I stood shaking with rage and searching the darkness, a car motor raced outside. There was a great wrenching and tearing sound. Woodwork gave way. What few remnants of unbroken glass were still left in the front of the house now fell out and shattered with a crash. Then a car was speeding away and I did not have to hunt through the ruins to know that I was alone. An almost unearthly quiet followed the sudden bedlam.

I moved carefully so as not to bring cracked and sagging plaster down around my head. Every step I took was hazardous. Glass crunched under foot and the stench of whiskey and rum and cordials was everywhere. The cold night air blew through the barroom—the whole front wall of the room was gone. Tables and chairs were broken, my office desk upturned and files spilled out upon the floor and soaked with whiskey. The proud marble rail in front of the bar and the brass rods that supported it had been ripped away. The mahogany itself had dozens of axe marks, and there was broken lath and plaster where the back-bar mirror had been.

I wondered what a man was supposed to do. I reached down behind the overturned desk. The phone was a lifeless thing. I dropped it amid the glass and the scattered papers and the pools of spilled liquor. I stepped carefully to where the door had been and out into the night.

I stood in the cool air, trying to breathe more slowly, trying to let my heart action slow a little. But I knew that I could not stand there for long, and finally turned toward the garage, got into my car and put the rifle, butt down, beside me. I backed the car out and turned carefully and drove across what had been the blue shale of the drive and parking area. The shale was no longer blue, except in spots. Someone had carefully smashed a barrel of oil where its contents would twist and wind across the neat drive and the parking area.

I reached the road and I thought that I was keeping remarkably good control of the car, myself, the situation. I knew what I should do. I should get to the nearest phone and call the troopers and the sheriff. But I also knew that they were far away and that time was important—I drove to General Gunther Cramer's house. And I wondered whom I should ask for first when I got there—for the two ex-MP's, for the general or for Anne Cramer?

The drive was a short one. The house was dark when I reached it. I went up the front steps and lifted the knocker. I found and pressed the button of the door chime. Such double-barreled action should have brought double-barreled results. But the mansion awoke slowly.

I must have looked a little like a madman, standing there clutching my rifle, when the housekeeper finally answered the door. She had thumbed on the porch light and opened the door, but only far enough to let it reach the end of the night chain.

"Who are you? What do you want?" she said, and then, seeing the rifle, she started to jam the door shut. I swung the gun butt up and wedged the door.

"I'm Jason Broome," I said. "I own River House. I want to see the general and his daughter. I want them to let me talk to the two friends of Major Craddock who are living here."

I heard the click of heels and Anne's voice said, "Is that really you, Jason?"

"It sure is. Let me in, Anne, and call your father."

A man's voice, deep and commanding, said, "Don't let anyone in. Keep that chain on the door. Stand back, you two. Let me see who's there."

We looked at each other across the small brass chain which allowed the door to be opened only a hand's width, the general and I. I saw a tall man in a purple dressing gown, shoulders braced, jaw prominent, eyes shrewd and bright with vitality. What he saw was less impressive, but just as stubborn.

I said, "My name is Jason Broome. You have two men here, General Cramer—acquaintances of the late Major Craddock. I want to talk to them."

The general got busy with the little brass chain. He said, "Come in, Broome. I've been hoping to see you, but hardly this soon. Naturally I expect that your message is urgent at this hour." He got the door unchained and I strode into the hall.

The housekeeper edged toward a door on the left as I entered, but Anne and her father stood their ground, facing me. Anne's face had an expression of alertness—I had the feeling that she was keyed up, tense, ready to jump. I also had the impression that she knew why I was here. There was no particular surprise on her face.

I addressed them both. "Until tonight I owned a place called River House. A few nights ago your two guests paid me an armed visit, which I didn't report to anyone. Anne, however, can corroborate the fact that they were there. Tonight someone just about ruined the place—and I just want to make sure your guests have been sleeping soundly."

General Cramer took a cigar out of the breast pocket of his dressing gown. He put it between his teeth and spoke around it. "I sent word to you today that I had a business proposition for you. I'm not sure that's true now, Broome. What in the hell do you mean shoving in here and demanding to question my guests about some vandalism undoubtedly perpetrated by the drunken patrons of your glorified saloon?"

I said to Anne, "Tell your father about the type of hoodlum he refers to as his guests."

Anne was wearing some sort of a red silk negligee that wasn't right for that golden hair. She looked both strange and familiar as she came forward and put a hand on my arm.

"Jason," she said, "you're wrong this time. I've been awake. No one could have gone out or come in without my hearing them."

"Maybe they didn't have to go out. Maybe they never came in from wherever they were earlier in the evening."

"But they've been here since dinner. Father had a conference with them in the library afterward. They're being briefed on a job they're to do—" there was a noise upstairs at that moment, and the two ex-MP's came to the railing and looked down.

"Anything wrong?" one of them said.

I couldn't see well enough to tell at that distance, in the dimly-lit upper corridor, whether his hair was tousled and his eyes sleep-swollen or not. I was beginning to have the feeling that either I had made a fool of myself by coming here, or would make one of myself by staying. Too late I realized that the devastation of River House would have required more than the strength and agility of two men.

But I hated to be bluffed, and there was one thing left that I could check before admitting momentary defeat. I said, "I'll apologize for the intrusion if you'll do me one favor."

"What is it you want, Jason?" This came from Anne— her father simply stared at me in frowning appraisal.

I said, "I'd like to visit your garage."

An explosion was shaping up. I could see it in the general's eyes, in the rush of blood to his face. But Anne touched his arm.

"Wait, Father. We'd best end this tonight, once and for all. Something has happened at River House, and he has the right to question us because of something that happened there once before. Please go to bed—and ask the boys to go, too." She turned to the housekeeper. She said, "Put the chain on the door, after we go out, then wait and let me in."

Her father said, "What do you think you're going to do, Anne?"

She said, "I'm going to settle an issue. I'm going to prove something to Jason, something he has to know before he can decide whether to come in with us or not." Her eyes clashed with her father's, and once again I was aware of the dominating side of her personality. "You do still want him to work for you, don't you?"

The general looked from one to the other of us, and I think he found meeting my eyes much the easier going. Finally he grunted something that Anne obviously took for acquiescence, for she patted his arm, smiled at him and turned to me.

"Come on, Jason."

MURDER WITHOUT TEARS

I opened the door for her, closed it on her still scowling father, and we were in the dimness of the porch. A floodlight flashed on almost instantly, lighting the grounds, and as we crossed the wide driveway to the garage, I had a feeling that the general—and perhaps his guests—were watching us with unfriendly interest.

Anne said, as we walked, "This time you've got to believe me—no one in this house is directly responsible for whatever happened at River House tonight. Do you want to tell me what did happen?"

I said, "Someone broke in and smashed the place—someone who knew just what to do. Do you remember my telling you how carefully your two friends reconnoitered the place the last time they called? They must have known the position of every bottle, every fixture—they even knew where I kept my private files. They wrecked the place in less time than it took me to wake up and rush downstairs."

Her voice was calm, assured. "You didn't tell me, but I was there, remember? I thought we were both agreed that they were looking for me—not reconnoitering, as you put it."

She had something there, and I felt my case against the men she had referred to her father to as "the boys" weakening. But stubbornly I said, "I'm not so sure now that they were looking for you, Anne."

She said it lightly, but there was an undertone of seriousness in her voice that warned me. "Do you think I came along as a decoy that night, to keep you from pursuit? To cover for the boys—give them a reason for coming to River House?"

I said, "I don't know what to think," and heard a small, shocked sound beside me. By now the hurt of what had happened to my pride and livelihood was really beginning to register, and I didn't look at her. We walked some moments in silence, and then I began to remember how she had been later that night in my arms, what we had said to each other—and suddenly I was ashamed of myself.

I said, "I'm sorry, Anne. I shouldn't have said that—I don't really think it. But something else happened at River House tonight, and that's the real reason I'm here."

She said, "What was that?" and her voice was cool and detached, as if nothing had ever occurred between us at all.

I looked at her and her eyes were neither cool nor detached—there was infinite hurt in them, and far down under the hurt, an infinite anger. I was a little startled, I think—and at that moment, more than ever before, I longed to take her in my arms and kiss away both her hurt and her anger.

But the general's floodlights bathed us—we were at the closed garage doors. She looked at me expectantly, waiting, and I said, "Just as they left—whoever they were—they pulled off the whole front wall of the bar. It takes special machinery to do that—an army man would know of such machinery. Craddock might have known—so might his two cronies, and your father, for that matter. Do you have a tractor or a heavy truck on the premises?"

She said, still in that quiet voice, "I think you had best see for yourself," and reached for the door handle.

I helped her raise the wide doors, and she switched on the garage lights. I saw three gleaming cars—the Buick, the Mercury, the major's Cadillac—and a battered and dusty Ford station wagon, probably used by the help and to run heavy errands.

Purely for the sake of the gesture, and to have something to do while I thought of how to straighten matters with Anne, I walked around each vehicle carefully, studying each for damage caused by recent violent use, feeling the radiator of each. None had been driven so recently as to enable me to detect any radiator warmth—nor was any one of these cars powered to do what had been done to River House, without suffering damage.

I came back to Anne at the door. Some of the hurt and anger had gone from her eyes, to be replaced by a sort of sadness.

But she said lightly enough, "Well—did you find any engines of war?"

I shook my head. I began, "Anne, I'd like to tell you how sorry I am—" but she cut me off with a gesture.

"Please skip it, Jason," she said tiredly. "You're sorry, and I am too, but in just a few moments you'll be thinking of something else—in fact you've probably already thought of it. You'll remember that Father's contractors have any number of trucks and tractors, and that machines that build can easily be made to destroy."

I had, as a matter of record, already thought of it. I stared at her in silence. She met my eyes for a moment, than turned away.

"We'd best get these doors closed," she said.

We closed the doors together and began the trek back to the main house in silence. We still walked in the general's floodlights, and anything I could say or wanted to say shriveled to insignificance in the bright glare.

Finally Anne spoke. "You hated the war, didn't you, Jason?" She waited a barely appreciable moment before going on. Then she said, "You thought it was merely destructive—well, so did my father—the general. He fought in the first one as a young man and liked it—he thought it achieved a purpose. Germany lost her kaiser and Russia her czar. The second war was fought against people, with new leaders. The leaders were wrong, but he saw only the destruction wrought against people—not little people, but people like you and me. Who were just trying to live. When he came back, he wanted to build—"

I said, "Did Craddock share his views?"

111

Anne was a little while answering. When she did, her voice was as quietly assured as before. "Craddock laughed at his views. Craddock loved the war—he'd been a small-time real estate speculator and a gambler before. The war made him. The war gave him more authority than he'd ever known. It made him a bigger man than he'd ever been. And after the war my father found that he could use him in his real estate developments."

"And to bulldoze people—as he bulldozed the land to put up little tarpaper-and-stick houses for little tarpaper-and-stick people? I never believed in those, Anne. That's why I bought River House."

We had reached the bottom of the porch steps in the bright glare. We paused and she turned to face me.

"He makes mistakes as all people do," she said. "I don't think he would make a mistake on you—or the River House."

I had nothing to say to that. We ascended the steps in silence and were halfway across the porch when suddenly the lights winked out.

We stood in an abrupt, stygian darkness and I heard a sudden sob beside me. Or perhaps it was more the catching of a breath. Then, suddenly, Anne was against me—my arms were about her and my lips found hers in the dark.

Our kiss was other than it had been. It began as the others had begun, as a mutual seeking for oneness beyond words—but gradually I sensed her withdrawal, grew aware of her body's trembling under my hands.

When her lips had grown cold and her arms lax, I released her. We still stood touching in the dark, and she whispered something I was not to understand fully till the end—till all the ties between us were broken.

"Jason," she breathed. "Jason, Jason—now I'm afraid—"

She moved away from me swiftly then. She knew, of course, much better than I, what she was doing—still

112

blinded by the recent glare of the floodlights, I had no idea of where she had gone, until I saw the dim glow beyond the half-open door. She was a swift shadow, passing through; the door closed again and I heard the snick of the chain that secured it.

I stood there some seconds, trying to find my bearings, mentally, emotionally, physically. Presently the last grew most urgent—I groped my way off the porch and, after a few false starts in the darkness, found my car.

As I switched on my headlights and the house and grounds remained dark, I didn't know whether to curse or bless whoever had thrown the switch that gave Anne and myself that last magic moment alone in the dark.

I didn't fret too much about it. My motor caught instantly; I swung around in the wide driveway and headed home—to what had been my River House.

12

THE ancient ruin of a Roman building has today only a tourist appeal that carries with it no shock of recent catastrophe. It all happened long ago. Time has given the ancient walls an aura of mellowness—the patina of the ages is like fresh white-wash, creating a new interest.

But the brand-new, immediate ruin of what was only yesterday an up-and-coming business is a sight without splendor. It might be a sensation for a day or two; and the curious would drive past to see it and to speculate. The police would investigate. Yet in my case a whole way of life had vanished for both employer and employees. I had put such profits as I made into improving River House—I had no reserves against cataclysm.

I steered clear of the wide-spreading pool of oil in the blue shale of the drive, parked the car and stood in the early dawn looking at the mess that had been left behind by whoever it was that had not wished me well. I picked my way through the debris, and wondered just how many men had moved what heavy equipment so quietly to accomplish such destruction as this. The front wall of the bar lay distorted in the drive, and the wreckage inside glinted balefully in the early light. The effectiveness of the raid suggested commando tactics, which brought me back to

114

Craddock, General Cramer—perhaps even to Anne. The only other possible tie-in was the vandalism perpetrated on Eloise Ruysdale's car—and mine was destruction on a much vaster scale. Besides, what was the connection between Eloise and myself, unless it was the murder of Craddock?

There my thoughts halted, and I saw no way of stirring them further. I decided on some rest before getting in touch with the police. Besides, from what I knew of Hoyle, he would probably be around any moment and try to tell me exactly what had happened.

I tested the stairs. Perhaps I only imagined that they felt shaky. I started up them, moving carefully, thinking that there was no longer reason to be half-alert at night, even while I tried to sleep. The worst had happened. I had had my visitors and I was finished. I could go to bed and let the deepest kind of sleep drug me away from reality for a little while.

There was a hot sun in my face when I awoke. I got up and crossed to the bathroom and drank two or three glasses of water. The upstairs plumbing at least, I remember thinking, had not been damaged. I took a shower and felt better. I put on slacks and loafers and a fresh sport shirt and went downstairs. I had not called the police, but as I reached the first floor, I saw a gray state police car skirting the pool of oil in the blue shale, and watched it pull up beside my car.

I went outside, and the first trooper out of the car said, "What the hell's been going on?"

I had missed Franz this morning—he was always the first to arrive to work—so I said, "Didn't Franz tell you?"

The trooper gave me a funny look. He said, "Your cook? He's the guy who reported this—said when he showed up for work this morning he found the whole place shot to hell and his boss asleep. He gave us a message to his boss—are you the guy?"

"I own River House," I said. "What's left of it."

The trooper looked at me through clear gray eyes, with some amusement in them. "The message is—he's quitting."

That was the first really reassuring thing I had heard in several days. The sunlight seemed suddenly a little warmer, and for the first time it seemed to me that my world might eventually come back to normal.

I said, "That's all right. Franz quits every time I come down for breakfast. The trouble is, I like to fry my own eggs." The trooper was very young, but an understanding half-grin twitched his features. I noticed his companion, half out of the car, was busy taking notes—they both looked young and hopeful. I said, "Perhaps you'd like to look around—and I'll tell you what I can."

We took a tour amidst the ruins, and I told them what I knew. I omitted all mention of Craddock and the Cramers, because I had come from there, frankly, last night, not knowing what to think. There was some trouble about my not having reported the trouble immediately, but Franz had saved me there. He had told them, while making his report, that lately I had been drinking immoderately.

When I explained, "The whole thing happened before I could wake up and come downstairs—and after that there seemed to be very little anyone could do until morning—" they exchanged understanding glances.

A short while later, after promising to be in touch, they left—and my next visitor that morning was Sue Prescott.

She was wearing sneakers, white wool socks, tennis shorts and a blouse to match. Her tanned face was almost expressionless, and I noticed for the first time that there was the faintest slant to her eyes, particularly in moments of stress. Evidently, I caused her stress.

From our last conversation, I had not expected to hear

116

from her directly, and somewhere in the back of my mind had been notions about lawyers and minor defalcations on local ordinances and other nuisance gestures—with murder and other things on my mind, I had not been taking Sue Prescott seriously as a threat. From the way my system did a wing-flip at the sight of her this morning, I surmised I might have been wrong. She was both brunette and beautiful.

She said, "I heard about this at the country club—now that I've decided to stay, I've taken a cottage there."

At the moment the only thing that registered was that she had heard about last night. The troopers had barely left —Anne, I thought, must be an early riser.

Then I noticed that she was looking past me, and realized that this devastation must mean something special to her, also, for River House had been her childhood home. So I told her the whole story.

She began to move past me even as I began. Together we wandered through the wrack and the ruin. And I told her the things I had not mentioned to the state troopers—about Craddock and Anne and the general. I even mentioned Hoyle and Howard Carter. The only thing I left out was the night Anne had actually spent with me at River House —after telling her about the night she had not spent there but had confessed to, to save both our necks from the noose.

When I had finished I thought there was shock in her eyes, for exactly what reason, I couldn't tell. I said nothing more then; without my realizing it, we had completed another tour of River House, and whatever I had done to it since it had been her home, more had been done to it now.

After some moments she spoke. "Jason—what are your plans now?"

I said, "I've been accused of murder. Right now I could commit one—if I could find out whose."

For the first time this morning she smiled. "That doesn't

sound as if you were anxious to start putting up cracker-barrel houses for General Cramer," and I agreed that it didn't.

We sat silent for some moments, with the day brightening about us and ruin and desolation all around.

Finally she said, "That view into the valley—do you suppose when you replace that wall, Jason, it could be glass? They do wonderful things with glass nowadays; they can make it as strong as steel. Then people who come here could see outside, as we're doing now, down to the river and—" She stopped abruptly, looking at me. A faint flush was on her cheeks, but her eyes were steady. "They could see where they were going, more or less—figuratively speaking—after they left here. Am I making sense?"

She was making sense. She was making more sense than anyone I had listened to in a long time—more than I had made to myself at any time about River House. For the first time, really, I saw the beautiful world beyond the broken wall—the steel gleam of the river, the green drop of the valley, the lovely bustle of living and livelihood that must always be the Hudson.

I said, "You're making sense—up to a point. The point is where my money runs out and River House begins. I don't know when I can start rebuilding the place, but you're right on one count—people should always have been able to look outward from here."

She was watching me quite seriously, that slight flush still on her cheeks, but deep in her warm brown eyes I could see the beginnings of fun and laughter.

She said, "It would spoil this place as you've had it. This wouldn't be again the barroom from the flats."

I met that look, and somewhere inside me there was laughter, too, not at either of us now, but at the way things had been. "No," I said. "It wouldn't. Nor would it be the place you grew up in," and suddenly we were both smiling and looking—not at each other, but outward through the broken wall. I thought I would probably never forget this moment. I said, "I'll remember this when I start rebuilding River House."

After a moment she asked very softly, "Would it cost a great deal of money, Jason?"

I told her, "Yes," and once more she looked squarely at me.

"I have a great deal of money," she said.

"Just what is that supposed to mean?"

"It means that I've thought things over since I last saw you. I've talked to people; you've made River House stand for something in this community. You've let in people who were never up on the hill before—they've mingled here with people they might never otherwise have met. I don't want to turn back time—I thought I wanted to change this house back to what it had once been, but it could never be that any more, could it, Jason?"

No, I thought, *and neither can you or I ever be again what we once were, and thank God for that!*

I said, "Are you proposing to invest in the restaurant and bar business, when you see the risks before you?" I nodded to the broken wall, the smashed interior of the place.

She smiled. "One of the people I talked to about you and River House was my lawyer. You may know him as one of your patrons—Charles Henlon. He thought it would be a wise investment, and I've never lost money with him yet."

I stared at her, and by God she meant it—every word! I stood up, suddenly restless, and walked out through the debris to what was left of the blue shale drive. Sue Prescott followed me.

I turned to her. I said, "I need time to think. Do you realize that right now you could buy River House for a song? I haven't the money to rebuild it—in other words, I couldn't lose by accepting your offer, but you could. While

we agree on one improvement, we might not agree on all—
you might be disappointed in the end result. River House
has to mean something else to you than it does to me—"

I stopped. There didn't seem anything else to say.

She looked at me very seriously, standing against that
backdrop of ruin.

She said just two words. "Must it?"

I stared at her and had no answer. There was a knowing
in her eyes, and she had been around—she had traveled
most of her life since leaving Newburyport. She had seen
a good many places since she had last seen her home, and
many of those places must have been what she had in mind
as she now thought of River House. I looked once again
at the valley and the view was magnificent—with the right
kind of money, the right kind of care and backing, River
House might be made into one of the showplaces of the
world.

I turned back to her to continue our discussion—perhaps
to end it—when there was a crunch of gravel near us, and
Anne's voice reached me.

"Forgive me if I'm intruding."

She was walking up the drive, picking her way through
the gummy pools of oil. She was smiling, not with her usual
gusto, not with her normal appreciation of life, but un-
certainly, as if she did not quite know what awaited her.

She reached us and surveyed the ruin. "Oh, Jason," she
said, not smiling at all now. "How perfectly ghastly!"

Sue and I had moved a little apart.

She said, "Jason and I have just been talking about it—
I think he ought to restore River House."

Anne's teeth caught her rich lower lip in the familiar expression. She frowned. "Can it be done?" she asked. "I
mean without its costing frightfully? Besides, I thought—"
her clear gray eyes pulled away from the house and probed
into mine—"I thought—didn't we have other plans, Jason?"

"I don't know," I said. I smiled at her. "How does your father feel about me this morning?"

"How should he feel? Of course you had a perfect right to disturb us last night—after all, what are neighbors for? In fact, he was wondering this morning what you were doing about breakfast and sent me to fetch you."

I said, "Thanks, but I think I can manage here. I think I'd better stick around—the state police were here earlier, a sort of first look around. They may be back. Too, some of the help will be showing up and I've got to talk to them."

Just then some of them did show up, and in a curious way I felt relieved. Anne I loved, of that I was still sure, despite my suspicions of the Cramer household regarding last night's doings, and Sue had just offered me an unforeseeable opportunity to restore to a greater beauty my other love, River House.

Yet the two were at cross purposes, for Anne wanted me to go to work with her father—and I wanted no wrangling here.

Not this morning. Not when I had so much to do.

13

THEY were clustered excitedly in the parking area, studying the wreckage that had been their livelihood. I saw
Armando standing a little apart from the others, and the
figure beside him made me grin. It was Franz.

Armando came over to me. He said, "What gives?" and
his face was thinner and the way his lips peeled back from
his teeth was an indication of the fury building inside him.

I said, "Night riders."

For a minute he may have had a vision of sheeted figures
on fast-moving horses, but he brought it up to date in a
hurry. "It took a truck to do that," he insisted. He whistled
a low note and shook his head and suddenly he had me by
the arm. "Let's go, boss. Who do we kill for this?"

He meant that. His eyes were flat in their sockets and
there was sweat on his pale upper lip.

I said, "I wish I knew. I feel that way, too."

He had not let go of my arm. He shook the arm a little.
"Let me make one guess," he said. "The dame. Somewhere
at the bottom of this the dame is mixed in. And Craddock
—why don't he stay dead?"

I turned to look. Anne was coming up behind us.

"Lay off," I said to Armando. "She isn't involved. You
know that. We're friends."

"Friends!" he said derisively. He let go of my arm. He backed off a little. I wondered if I was going to have trouble with him, but all he said was, "I guess you're finished here."

"For now, at least," I said. "I don't know if I can raise the money to rebuild and refurnish. And if I can—it will take the rest of the summer. I'm sorry, Armando. I'll send you a two weeks' check. Tell the others."

I was surprised to see how much trouble he had in swallowing. He said, "It's not losing the lousy job that cuts me up. It's the idea that somebody could do this to us and get away with it. We had a nice place here."

I said, "Thanks, kid. I know. And I know I could count on you if I could finger the guilty parties. But I can't, so we write it off—like a fire or an earthquake or an explosion."

Armando said, "I better tell the chef and the other boys. Jobs are open in the mountains now." He put out his hand. "If you ever find out who did this—maybe you'll send for me. I'd like to be with you when you call on them."

"Thanks, Armando."

"I mean it, boss. So help me. And one other thing—you notice I ain't asking questions. But advice I'm giving out with." He glanced over my shoulder and said quickly, "That dame back there—"

I said, "Maybe we ought to skip the dame."

"Like hell! When did all this trouble start? When you met her! I'm going to say this. Don't try to shut me up. That dame is poison. I've seen 'em like her before. I bet she's got a job all lined up for you to go to. A job where she'll be boss, no matter who signs the paycheck."

I am always going to be surprised by people like Armando. Where it had taken me days of intimate acquaintance with Anne to discover her domineering qualities, he seemed to be reading her like a book, at a few glances. Guys like that must lead wonderfully successful love lives.

But what I said was, "You're over your head now, kid.

Skip it. Tell the others they can expect at least two weeks' pay. If I can get backing for rebuilding, I'll let them know. Maybe we'll all be in the same boat again."

Armando grinned at that and I was grateful, for the joke was feeble.

He said, "You bet, boss," and left me.

I walked back to where Anne and Sue were still talking. Sue said, "I'm sorry that I didn't know about your earlier job offer, Jason. I wasn't trying to hire you away."

I said a little irritably, "I wasn't aware that I had put myself on the block. I'm certainly not committed to anything, Sue."

For a quick instant her eyes were angry. She looked past me at Anne. She said, "I thought—" and didn't finish the sentence. Her face was suddenly a mask.

Anne said, "I'm sorry if there's been a misunderstanding. Father did make the offer to Jason. We both thought a position with the Cramer enterprises would offer more of a future than running a small town roadhouse."

I said, "It would undoubtedly take me off the hot spot in Major Craddock's murder. Conceivably it might some day make me a United States Senator."

Anne had the grace to blush. Sue, not understanding my reference, looked from one to the other of us, bewildered.

Finally Sue held out her hand. "I'm going back to the cottage and get some sleep," she said. "I'm not trying to persuade you to do anything you don't want to do, Jason. But you can let me know your decision later."

Anne smiled politely and said that she would be seeing Sue around. She stood there with me and watched Sue drive away. Then she said, "She's pitifully unsure of what she wants, isn't she?"

I said, "Were you ever that way?"

She gave me a quick sharp look. After a moment she said,

"No—and I wouldn't like to be tied to a man who was." Her eyes when she looked at me were gambler's eyes. Take it or leave it.

I can be a gambler too—I chose to leave it. I said, "To hell with all this, Anne. Let's take first things first. We're still mixed up with murder. Did you know the state police have seen through your clever scheme for switching tires? They're checking every gas station tire purchase in the county. I hope you remembered to wear a mustache or disfigure yourself when you made some of those buys."

I thought she paled a little—I hoped at least to make some kind of impression. I do know that her eyes narrowed.

Finally she said, "All right, so I've bought new tires. They'll still have to find the old ones and trace them to me before they can place us in the brickyards."

I had been waiting for thas "us" to tie me also to those tire marks at the pit. Until now they had been her tires and she had disposed of them at will. But now that I was accepted as an equal partner under the incriminating evidence, I found myself not minding too much.

I smiled at her. We were learning things about each other —perhaps only the things every boy and girl should know. I wasn't sure.

I said, "I think you're absolutely right, Anne. And since we don't have to worry about those tire marks for the moment, maybe I'd better start straightening up here."

She looked helplessly at the mess around us. "What can you possibly do?"

"I can get this place boarded up to keep the sightseers out. Then I'll be over for a talk with the general."

She laughed at me. She said, "There you go—I invited you to a breakfast business conference that could make your future. But you'd rather work with your hands to protect something you've lost."

I said, "Right now I'm the cheapest unemployed labor that I know of."

"Right you are, Jason! And you'll stay just that, if you don't get out of your rut. Come to work for father and a half hour later a full crew of men will be here boarding up River House. That's organization."

I looked at my hands. It had been a long while since the brickyard days. My hands were soft, my muscles would be soft too. I thought, *What have I got to lose?*

"Well, Jason?" she said.

I made the decision. I said, "I'll follow you in my car."

Her smile was something new. It was well bred and quiet, but what it reminded me of was the victory cry of some jungle animal.

Anne drove fast—and when we reached the Cramer house, I could tell why. The general was pacing the porch.

Anne went up to him hurriedly and said, "We were delayed, father. Jason had to tell his men what happened and dismiss them."

He said, "I see." He examined me as thoroughly as if this were the first time that he had ever seen me. I wondered if he thought a man looked better or worse in the daylight.

I said, "Good morning," and felt myself bristling. There was trouble here.

He said, "Good morning, Broome," in a begrudging voice. "My daughter feels that there are some matters that you and I should talk over. But breakfast is waiting."

We went in and down the hall to the breakfast room. It was pretty formal—drapes and dark colors and old, old furniture. I preferred such modernizations as I had made in River House as it had been.

Breakfast seemed to be a silent ritual. When it was ended the general said to the maid, "We'll have fresh coffee in

my study," and excused himself to Anne. He said to me,
"Come along, Broome," and led me out and down the hall
to a room filled with metal filing cabinets and oak desks
and telephones. Just the number of phones gave me a
glimpse of the size of the general's dream.

He waved me to a chair, took his place behind the desk
and said, "What does this remind you of, Broome?"

I made it as succinct as I could without offending a
general. I said, "G.H.Q., sir."

"Exactly." General Cramer smiled at me. "I was hoping
you would see it as my new War Room. A peacetime war,
to be sure—but the heart of a great organization throbs
here."

I said, "Yes sir."

"Broome," he said, and lit a cigar, "my daughter thinks
that you could be an asset to our organization. She feels
that you could handle the late Major Craddock's job."

I said, "I'm afraid that I haven't had any specialized
training for it."

He said, "Nonsense. You were an officer in the war,
weren't you? A trained man. One of us. You would do
nicely, I think—after the proper orientation."

I looked at his shirt front and thought of orientation. The
infallible way to make a man believe anything.

I said, "Thank you, sir," and waited.

"Briefly," he said, "I need a contact man with my contractors. We have no direct labor trouble. We generally
operate in areas where construction is limited to our opera-
tion and when we employ local artisans, their business agents
determine the wage scale."

He let that hang awhile, but I caught on almost immediately. I had come out of the brickyards. I was not very
union-conscious, but I knew about unions. I saw no need
to express an opinion.

He must have seen that I understood. "You would move

in here, pick up the routine—be available for whatever duties needed performance."

Since he had decided to be blunt about it, I thought I might follow suit.

I said, "How many heads would I have to crack in the course of a year? I've heard some of these small-time contractors have pretty thick bones."

That got to him right where he lived. His glare vanished, he smiled. "We'll start slowly. How many cracked heads would ten thousand a year buy?" He actually chuckled, a rumbling noise like a mortar shell. "No need for you to name a figure—you'll know when rough tactics become necessary. You'll be allowed all travel expenses, of course."

"I'm not dickering. But there's the question of personal satisfaction in a job. I don't know how well I could earn my money here."

"What's your other alternative? Restore River House?"

"Yes."

"Can you get financing?"

"I believe so."

"And then what will you have? Just another pretentious saloon."

"But I'll be my own man. If I must crack heads, I choose whose."

He thought about that. The thinking cost him no pain— he was smiling. "From what I've heard lately, 'whose' seems to be your main problem. Any idea as yet about who did you in?"

"I'm not sure about being done in," I said. "But nevertheless, I've no more idea than I did last night about who destroyed my property."

That did away with his smile. He rumbled, "Now, see here, Broome—I'll have no more of insinuations such as you made last night."

I smiled. "I'm not sure that I blame you. I wouldn't like them myself."

For seconds the Jovian thunder gathered on his brow, and I braced myself for lightning. Nothing happened. The brow cleared. A second rumble started in that deep, military chest, exploded in soft laughter that shook the walls.

"By God, Broome, you've got gall. I'll bet you'd be willing to take a job with me, while thinking me your worst enemy." He leaned across the desk, cigar in hand, and an expression of honest interest in his strong, craggy face. "Tell me, what would you do to the man responsible for ruining your place, if you caught him?"

I said quietly, "Kill him if I could. He destroyed more than River House. He ruined the livelihood of a number of people whose only crime was working for me. If I couldn't safely kill him, I would turn him over to the authorities—but I would try my best to kill him first."

General Cramer leaned back. He put the cigar into his mouth and said past it, "I'll be perfectly frank with you, Broome. Hiring you was more Anne's idea than mine. But judging from your answer to that last question, I think she may have made a good choice. I wish you'd give my offer very careful thought."

I stood up. "Thanks very much, sir, I'll certainly think things over."

A phone began to ring, then another. He picked up the nearest and nodded. "Come back when you're ready with a decision, Broome. Good day, now."

I closed the door behind me and went down the corridor. Anne was waiting near the front door. She was smoking a cigarette.

She said, "I didn't hear him shouting. Are you two going to get along?"

"I'm not sure about the future," I said. "But so far we get along."

The quick, surprising anger was again in her eyes. "Don't be a fool, Jason," she said. Then, as abruptly, she smiled and came closer to me, until I could almost feel the warmth of her. "If you're worried about closing up River House, I had one of father's crews sent over while you were talking with him."

"You shouldn't have done that, Anne."

"Why not?"

"Because nothing is definite yet." Actually I was wondering whether this was the same crew that had wrecked River House last night. The nearness of her was a heady thing, even at this hour of the day, but I was suddenly uneasy and restless. The reach of her arm around my neck, the pressure of her hand at my nape was like the closing of a gentle trap. I pulled away.

"Let's get out of here, Anne. I want to take a drive—think this over."

She said, "We can combine business with pleasure. There's some trouble coming up about a hotel we're building on the Jersey shore. I'd thought of driving down there. Why don't you come along?"

That, I thought, was the damnedest part of this whole setup —the main idea seemed to be "Come along, Jason." I hadn't worked to build up economic independence for this. And though she and everyone else seemed to have forgotten it, behind the whole rat-race lurked murder.

By way of reminding her, I said, "There's still the Craddock investigation—there's still Hoyle. I told you that the police were checking on that business of changing tires. Don't you realize that they might have the right answer by now?"

She looked at me oddly, with total unconcern. "Don't you understand yet that the police aren't ever going to have the right answer?"

I couldn't believe that. I said, "Once the business of Craddock's murder is cleared up, I'll know much better how to plan our future."

She laughed at me silently—it was the first time I had ever actually seen anyone do that.

She said, "In that case you really don't have much choice, darling. If you come in with Father, you'll automatically be clear of suspicion—and so will I. If you decide to continue with River House—" she shrugged—"well, you've already had a taste of it. The police are not the only people you'll have to worry about. Major Craddock had his enemies—but he also had very loyal friends."

I can be stubborn when I want to. I said, "I don't want to talk about it here, in this house. Here everything seems bought and pat—I might even sell myself for something less than I'm worth. I want you to take a drive with me, but not to the Jersey shore. I want to go down to the brickyards."

She stared at me. "What on earth for?"

I said very gravely, "That's where I first learned to think, Anne. That's where I came from—you'll have no advantage over me there. I want you to go down there with me—as you did the first time."

She laughed again. "Why, Jason, you almost sound afraid of me. Of course we'll go down there—just like the first time."

She linked her arm through mine, and despite the slight mockery implied in her words—as though she were humoring a child—I felt a warmth coursing through me at her touch, at the occasionally fleeting brush of her hip against mine as we went through the door and out.

We took her car. She drove past River House and, as she had predicted, carpenters were already at work boarding up the gaping holes. I felt strangely impersonal toward the sight, as though the place no longer belonged to me—

actually, of course, Anne had again taken charge. When we turned into the lane and bumped past the clay pit where Craddock had died, I wondered what had prompted me to come back to the scene. There had been a compulsion—actuated neither by morbidity nor guilt—but I could not define it.

It was only when we were getting out of the car that I had the full answer. I found myself watching Anne with an intensity that surprised me. When I tried to analyze it, I found myself remembering her earlier, almost unwholesome fascination with the apparent life under the surface, the sunken cart on the underwater road, the silent, dead houses lining the liquid streets. What had been her comparison—ancient Pompeii?

I watched her now and none of that former almost morbid interest showed on her face—she was just a pretty girl looking into a pond, with the sun on her, the water ripples reflecting on her face and the soft summer breeze molding her light dress to her magnificent body.

After a while she said, "Well, Jason, have you found what you came for?"

"I've found a pretty girl," I said and she laughed.

I took her hand and we walked along a path chalked red with brick shards. I said, "The first time we were here you were looking for a lost civilization."

She laughed again. "I'm my father's daughter. The general has always been a great student of history. Most military men are. Tell me, why did you really bring me here?"

"I thought we might discover something that's been over-looked."

Her fingers were suddenly lax in mine; I thought her breath caught.

She said, "Overlooked by whom—the police or us?"

I said, "Either."

But there was the first-person plural again, linking us together, and this time it made me uneasy. I felt her hand grow cool in mine and finally withdraw. We walked along in silence, side by side.

She spoke and, try as I might, I could detect no tremor of concern in her voice.

"You're taking this too seriously, Jason. Craddock doesn't concern us any longer. You're too normal. Because you've never had police trouble before you're letting one incident with them bother you too much."

"That incident happened to deal with murder. Actually that hasn't been what's bothering me. What I'm wondering about is the blackjack I'm supposed to have threatened Craddock with."

She asked, "Didn't you?" And then: "What else about the blackjack?" There was now a definite edge to her voice.

"I still have it."

Until now there had been no tension between us—as I glanced at her, I could see her stiffen visibly. Her calmness was gone. After a moment her hand once more sought mine, but her fingers were cold now and their movement mechanical, steely.

"How did you avoid giving it to them? Did you hide it?"

I said, "No. They just never asked for it." She didn't say anything for a minute. We were once again holding hands, her fingers laced tightly, coldly with mine. We kept walking and I tried to see her face. But her face was away from me now, her head bent a little. She was looking at the ground, and we walked on that way. We walked along the edge of the clay pit. There was no shelving beach, no shore. They had dug straight down, seeking out the clay, and the walls of the pit were almost perpendicular. Suddenly I sensed a fear between us and held tightly to her hand, and it was no place for us to be.

133

I said, "Let's get out of here."

She was ready and we went back to the car. I knew no more than I had known when we came here. But she knew a great deal more. She knew that although they had questioned me the police were not interested in the blackjack which had first made me a suspect.

14

WHEN we got back to the Cramer house there was a state police car in the driveway. Anne saw it as soon as I did—I could tell by the sudden drag of her tires.

She said lightly, "Company's come."

I recognized the B. C. I. man waiting on the porch. He got up and came toward us. He was looking at me.

"We've found the truck that wrecked your place, Broome. Had any trouble with a garage? It was a tow truck with a push plate—just the job for a wrecking car."

I got the irony of his words. I said, "I don't know any garage people. Where I buy gas they don't own a wrecker."

"Not this one, anyway. It was hot—stolen off a used car lot. We found it ditched on the edge of town. Can you tell us anything, from this new angle?"

"I'm sorry—nothing. It was stolen especially for the job?"

"That's our thinking. Well, I'll shove off, then. We hoped maybe the mechanic angle would fit. But it looks cold now. Sure you never threw a garageman out for getting noisy?"

"I'm sure. I'm also sure no customer of River House would want to wreck the place. You've got a bad deal. No motive, no suspect, and not much help from me. How about prints?"

He said, "We're trying. But it's a long chance."

I hesitated. "Anything else new?"

"You mean on Craddock? You wouldn't expect me to tell you, would you?"

I said, "It's still the big news. I can spend a dime and find out."

"You do that." He grinned. "I'll see you, Broome. By the way—remember Hoyle's phone tip about a guy named Howard Carter?"

I said, "Yes—" and suddenly I didn't think that the state police had come here to tell me about the ditched truck.

"He wasn't in town. He was in California that night and can prove it."

I said, "So you were able to check on that?"

"Easy. The county boys had a prisoner to be returned to California, and Hoyle delivered him. While he was there he checked on the Carter business at first hand."

Anne, at my elbow, made a small sound of surprise or disbelief, but when I turned to her, her features were controlled. She looked pale and drawn, though.

"If you don't mind, Jason," she said, "I won't ask you to lunch. I seem to have a terrific headache."

I said, "Not at all, darling. I've got to get home anyway." I turned to the trooper. "By the way, how did you know I was here?"

"Some workmen on your place said you might be at the general's—and while we're on that, I'm sorry as hell about what's happened. The wife and I've enjoyed a few of your Sunday dinners. Hope you open again soon."

I said, "Thanks," and he gave an informal salute and strolled back to his car.

I went with Anne to her door, then got into my car and drove back to River House.

*   *   *

136

When I got there a crew of men were quitting. The lower floor of River House was sided up like the false front on a demolition job. There was even a door in the siding. When I identified myself to the foreman, he handed me a key to the padlock that hung from the hasp.

I said, "This was sure a fast job."

"We just boarded it up. The mess is all there inside the false front."

I said, "Even so, it will keep the curious out."

He gave me a look that was not quite respectful, but rather curious. He said, "Miss Anne mentioned that you were coming with the company. We tried to do you a good job." I recognized the effort to get on the influence track. I let it be. There was no point in committing myself one way or the other.

I unlocked the padlock, opened the makeshift door and stepped into the wreckage beyond. My room seemed undisturbed. I went in and stretched out on the bed. As usual, I had some things to think about.

The first of these—lunch—I dismissed as being too prosaic and practical and too much trouble. Then I delved into what I could recall of my interview with the general and the practical aspects of his job offer. I tailed off into my talk with Anne about our future and the Craddock murder, and was just about to take up the matter of Sue Prescott and her partnership offer on River House, when I heard a light step on the stairs.

It was indicative of my state of mind that I instantly thought of Anne, and as instantly swore softly. I loved Anne, or thought I did, but she made strong emotional and mental demands on me, and was about the last person I wanted to see right now. My morning with her had been exhausting.

But when I got to the door of my room, it was not Anne I saw ascending the stairs, but Sue Prescott. She seemed

137

astonished to see me. "Jason—I was told you were staying at the Cramers'!"

I grinned wryly. "I had a breakfast interview with the general and was uninvited for lunch. This sad and sagging place is still my home. Won't you come up? The plaster's not falling up here, though these stairs you're standing on might collapse any moment."

She gaped at me, then gave an apprehensive look at the stairs. Suddenly she burst into laughter, looking up at me. It was the first time I had heard her laugh since we were children, and the sound was rich and pleasant.

She said, "I never heard a more sinister invitation in my life, but I am afraid of falling plaster and falling stairs. Are you sure I'll get down again?"

"We can always call the fire department," I said.

Then she sobered and came up.

"Please don't think I'm spying," she said. "Because I am. I was thinking of the deal I offered you this morning and, thinking that you were away, I came over for another look." Her brown eyes met mine candidly. She said, "I know something about investments, Jason. My father was in ill health for years, and knew that he was dying. He also knew that he was leaving me a considerable fortune, and went to some pains to teach me how to handle it. He told me about people and places and how to judge them."

She paused and it seemed up to me to say something. I said it.

"So?"

She colored a little. "So my offer still stands. I'll either buy River House from you, or back you with the capital you need to remodel. The first floor's sound enough—"

At this point she became aware of my grin and stopped.

I said, "Speaking of the first floor, that's where the kitchen is. Until you came along, lunch seemed a waste of time. Now we can make it business, if you'll join me."

I liked the way her eyes looked when she smiled—they seemed to have the world's warmth in them.

"I believe I could use a bite," she said, "if we can trust these stairs."

"One at a time," I said. "You first—I'm heavier."

Lunch proved to be more of an undertaking than I had figured. Some of the refrigerators were defrosted and the huge walk-in case had gone off power early in the game. But I had had a panel of throw-out switches installed because of the power load I was carrying at River House, and because house power was still on through the master switch, I was able to find one refrigerator that had not kicked off at the time of the smash-up. It was sheer chance that we found inside the case a whole cold roast chicken.

We made a feast. I found wine, and vegetables for a salad, and a full box of potato chips. The ice cream case had not kicked off, either. We shoved debris from a table in the corner of the dining room and lunched informally but very well.

Dined would be a better word. The sun was long gone behind the hill that backdropped the view, and by the time we had finished I was beginning to wonder how safe it would be to start testing the lights.

We had not talked a great deal, during dinner. We seemed to have reached the point where conversation was not really necessary. The silences between us had ceased to be embarrassing. But when she had finished her ice cream, she said, "There! That was wonderful. But if there was no water for the coffee, how can we do the dishes?"

I said, "I'm sorry—I never thought. The water's on upstairs. This pump is just for the kitchen, a special well. But doing dishes in a ruin like this would be the height of something pretty foolish."

She looked around the room, shadowy now with dusk.

"I know," she said. "It's the last little indignity that the

139

old house must suffer—we walk away and leave dirty dishes behind us."

I was a little drunk with the occasion. I said, "Whatever happens, I'm sending a crew in here to pick up the pieces. If I don't rebuild River House, at least I won't leave litter behind me."

She didn't answer for a moment. At last she said, "Jason —that must be the moon coming up. The wooden wall they built around the front of this place this morning is what makes it so dark in here. I think if we went outside we could see the moon rise across the river."

I said, "All right," and was mildly surprised at my own eagerness.

We went out together, hooking the padlock through the hasp but not locking it. We walked across the ruined gravel of the parking lot, crossed the road and stood with elbows touching, looking down upon the river valley, upon the brickyard flats and the old clay pit and the remnants of a way of life that was gone forever from this part of the earth.

Neither of us heard the car until it stopped on the road behind us. When we turned we saw it was the green Mercury and although we could not see her face by moonlight at that distance we knew that Anne was at the wheel and that she was looking at us.

We turned toward the car, not hurrying, and although there was no reason for me to feel guilt I felt it anyway. Not once during the afternoon and evening had I thought of her.

As we approached, Anne moved the car off the road, running it forward a little and then backing it off the shoulder onto the grass. There was something about the way that she did it, a certain choppiness, that indicated her mood. She got out then, and came toward us, and said abruptly: "Has that county detective, Hoyle, been out here?"

I said, "No, why? Are you looking for him? Has something happened?"

She said quickly, nervously, "I'm not looking for him. But he's been snooping around. He was over at the house twice this afternoon. They sent him away. It wouldn't surprise me if he knew they lied and came back with a search warrant. It must be about this Howard Carter. You remember that someone tipped Hoyle off by phone that Carter was seen in town the night the major was murdered?"

"I remember," I said. "You told Hoyle that you hadn't seen Carter—that you had no information about him other than the fact that he and Craddock had had trouble in Chicago."

She said, "Then why couldn't they leave it like that? Why did Hoyle have to go snooping around out in California, trying to prove that I had lied, that Carter had been here?"

I remember thinking that there was something strange about Anne that night—at the time I thought she was simply excited.

I said, "I don't think he was trying to prove that, Anne. I think he was trying to prove that you had told the truth— that you hadn't seen Carter. If he found proof that Carter was in California on the night of Craddock's murder it only confirmed what you had said."

She had moved quite close. She studied me carefully. For the moment she ignored Sue Prescott. She said, "Then you haven't seen Hoyle? He hasn't been out here?"

I said, "No. We've been talking for quite a while. Sue is thinking of buying River House, whether or not I take over the job of restoring it."

"But you can't!" she said. "It was all settled that you were coming with us."

"No it wasn't. Your father and I didn't come to any definite agreement."

"But that was just part of the negotiating—you were trying for more money than he offered."

"Money had no bearing on it. It happens I like River House. I always have."

Anne said, "I see—of course." Her voice was smooth and steady, but it still had that strange undertone of excitement. "I can understand that. It would be part of the ambition of little Jason Broome—the ambition to move up from the brickyard flats."

"I made that move long ago, Anne."

She thought about it. Then she nodded. "I guess you did, Jason."

Her gaze was steady on me and so concentrated that Sue might not have been there at all. Yet I wasn't sure that she saw me at all—her mind seemed to be grappling with some other problem, perhaps several of them.

When she spoke, her words had nothing to do with what had been said before.

She said, "It hardly seems likely that the police, even with their organization, will ever know who smashed River House. There isn't anything about a stolen truck to identify the thief; and even if there were fingerprints, what would they mean if they had never been recorded?"

I said, "You're absolutely right, Anne."

But for the first time then, Sue interrupted. She said, "Did you know that the police got prints at Eloise's garage the night her car was damaged? That's what frightened her off to Arizona. She was afraid that she might have to testify if the police could match the prints—she was afraid of whom she might have to testify against."

Anne smiled a little. She said, "Afraid it might have been some of her friends?" It was a good catty remark and she purred it. But then she said, "Really now—wouldn't the person who did that job have had sense enough to wear gloves? I'm sure that I would have. How about you, Sue?"

Sue said, "I'm not so sure." She glanced at me—I think she, too, had begun to see something a little strange about Anne. She moved almost imperceptibly closer to me.

Anne said lightly, making it an obvious joke, "Then you had better stay away from that young man from the state police. They tell me he's a wizard at fingerprints."

Sue's tone matched Anne's, but her words puzzled me. "Maybe I knew what I was doing when I tried to talk Jason into going to Arizona, too."

As though this were something between them that they alone understood, they spoke across me now.

Anne said, "I suspected that was what was going on. You might have made the trip with Eloise, as originally planned, if it hadn't been for the new development."

I tried to figure what the new development was. Sue seemed to understand. She said coolly, taking her time about it, spacing her words, "That was exactly it."

Anne shrugged. "I should be going home. I came out to see if Jason had had dinner. We were dining late tonight."

I said, "Thanks, Anne—but I rustled up a little food."

To my surprise, she let the matter drop—I remembered how urgent she had been this morning that her father and I get together. What had happened in the meantime to change her mind? Once again I had the feeling that her presence here was merely physical, that her thoughts and attention were elsewhere. Was Hoyle's return from California in some way connected with her distracted state of mind? Had there been any significance to Sue's remark about fingerprints on Eloise's car, and to the subsequent almost mystic exchange between Anne and Sue?

I was watching Anne, but she seemed to have forgotten me. She was looking toward the river. I remembered the night was breath-takingly beautiful and, physically at least, Anne did nothing to mar the scene. The moonlight that silvered the river and flooded the valley played on her

143

golden hair and limned her perfect figure, as she stepped past me and crossed the road to where Sue and I had been sitting some moments before. Abruptly I realized that her face was not the face with which I was familiar, nor her slow step the jaunty gait I had known and admired. I was aware of shock—she moved like one dedicated, like some priestess on her way to a forbidden rite. I half-expected, because of the look on her face, that the moonglow would draw her to the edge of the little plateau—and over.

I nearly rushed after her, but then she stopped. She simply walked to the edge of the drop and looked down at the river and at the railroad tracks and at the old brickyard flats. Then she said something I couldn't hear, nor did Sue Prescott. Sue was standing close beside me. She turned and I could see the question on her face.

I called, "What was that again, Anne?"

Anne said, "There's someone down by the clay pit, down where they found the major's body. Do you think we should go down and see?"

It was a macabre moment. Despite the night's warmth I felt a chill, and beside me Sue shivered. There had been something in Anne's voice—a high-pitched tension, like the hum of a wire stretched to the breaking-point. It carried an eerie conviction, and I for one was ready to believe that Anne somehow was witnessing the return of a murderer to the scene of his crime.

Anne's voice came again, pitched to the same eldritch key. "I see a light down there—it's moving slowly, as if someone—someone is looking for something." She stopped, turned and came toward us. "I think we should go down and see," she said.

I went past her to the spot where she had stood and looked down. I could see nothing, neither a light nor a movement.

I called back to Anne, "Are you sure you saw someone?" and she said in the same high strange voice, "Of course

I'm sure. Shouldn't we go down and see what's going on?"

I went back to the girls. "Going down there at night could be dangerous," I said.

Anne turned to face me fully in the moonlight. Her expression was wan, thinned-out, it almost looked like a trick of lighting.

"Of course it could be dangerous," she said. She added decisively, "You're not afraid on your own account, but because of Sue and myself."

I said, "I'm afraid on my own account, too. Let's be smart. It could be anyone down there from a bunch of kids to a maniac—" For the first time it came to me that perhaps Craddock had been killed by a madman—perhaps that was why the police had made so little headway in the case.

It was Sue who decided it for us. Sue said in her mild, casual voice, "I'm in favor of going down there. We're all more or less involved in what's been going on, and I'd rather face danger and know it than wait for the sort of thing that happened to Eloise and Jason."

When she put it like that, the proposal made sense. Besides, Anne was already in her car and had started the motor —I certainly had no intention of letting her go down alone.

The familiar road to the brickyard flats tonight was a black tunnel under interlacing tree branches, through which the moonlight filtered an intricate pattern, unreal, white and cold. I doubt that any of us really expected to find Major Craddock's murderer at the clay pit. In retrospect, I wonder what actually moved us to go down there—unless it was the strange conviction in Anne's keyed-up voice, her odd behavior; she was like some ancient seeress prophesying from an inner vision—and yet I can't recall a single thing she said or did that didn't belong to her time or place, the midpoint of the twentieth century, here and now, in the Hudson Valley.

We came out from under the tunnel of trees and the vista

of the flats and hard by the river made a dark pattern before us. Cloud scud was beginning to whip up and race across the face of the moon now, and each time that the moon was dimmed, the silvery pattern was smudged with gray, or became a sullen black mass without highlight or shadow.

Anne drove slowly along the river road, the car's motor a whisper on the night air, her headlights suddenly blacked out. As a matter of later record, she thought of the last herself, without a word from Sue or me. She seemed to find her way on the darkened road by instinct rather than sight— reasonable or not, I think we all three felt we were creeping up on a killer.

I remember thinking, "If there had been anyone here, he would have seen us come down the hill, blackout or not." But I sensed a real danger around us, and some of the perverse thrill of a hunter going after dangerous game. Sue had expressed some of what I felt when she had suggested our coming down here, and somehow now I felt a closer understanding with her than I did with Anne. There was a detached quality about Anne tonight, an aura of dedication seemed to surround her, and though we had loved, I sensed that tonight she was beyond love, beyond reach, with a purpose all her own.

Perhaps, I remember thinking, she had always been beyond my reach. Perhaps all of us are born for one purpose only, for one climactic moment for which we are equipped, a moment no one can take from us, the moment for which we are supremely talented.

Anne snaked the car along that dark, deceptive road with an easy assurance which, that night, I took for granted, but which, since then, I've remembered with awe. I thought even then that she must have been over this road a thousand times before she and I made our first visit to the clay pit. I had no thought of her duplicity then—I was simply grateful when a fender missed the black bulk of a tree, when we failed to drop down some dark declivity.

Finally, deftly, she pulled to the side of the road and parked. She killed the engine. Sue had been riding between us, and as though we knew her intent without being told, I opened the door on my side and Sue and I got out, as Anne slipped from behind the wheel on hers.

Our alignment was without forethought, and for the first time Anne seemed to become aware of it as she faced us across the hood. She stared, and for the first time also seemed uncertain.

Her eyes moved from one to the other of us and, "Well?" she demanded.

Her face was not as I remembered it—it was lovely still, well-boned and compact, but the eyes held the suspicion of a creature of the wild. Sue and I, as persons, had ceased to exist for her—I think a good many relationships she had lived by had, for her, ceased to exist.

Her mind was leaping impossible chasms, like a frightened chamois I had seen in the Alps during the war, when men were only hunting men.

She said without preamble, "Do you think I don't know what people have been saying? Or at least thinking—even if they didn't dare say it without proof? They're thinking I killed Major Craddock."

It was an incongruous scene we played in the fitful moonlight. Sue was very still beside me—Anne had the leading role. I found myself speaking lines that might have been written by Anne—of all the women I have known, I think she had the strongest flair for dominating a situation. Even then—even that night when she had dropped her defenses, when she should have been weakest.

I found myself playing to her cue. "Why do people think that, Anne?"

She said dispassionately, "Because I had the motive. You

147

didn't know this, but he and I were married. Secretly. We quarreled a great deal. If you read the papers, every time married people quarrel, there's a murder. Actually, it isn't like that. People live and love and fight together—I didn't kill Major Craddock."

I said, "Then who did, Anne?" And those too were only words she had managed into the scene for me, my lines in her production, giving no outlet to the blank, numb surprise —yes, and jealousy too—that I felt at the revelation. For a moment, Craddock lived again—Craddock of the thick neck and mannerless manners—Craddock and my girl. Married. Her golden warmth—and the major. Then once more he died for me, and pulled us all by his death into this pit with its mangy moonlight. Wandering . . . possibly lost . . . and my words still hung in the air while all this happened. *Then who did, Anne?*

A measure of caution veiled her eyes, and with it, a kind of sanity. "That's what we came down here to find out," she said. "Isn't it?"

It was, of course. As incredible as it now sounds, finding the killer of Major Craddock was what had brought us to the moon- and death-filled flats. And suddenly I cursed myself silently for having come here with two defenseless girls.

We had spoken quietly and the night was silent around us, yet I felt a pressure in the darkness that was almost tangible. Until now, I had been going along under Anne's unreal domination of the unreal scene—I don't think I had fully believed she had seen a prowler on the flats until now; her declaration up on the hill had had the quality of a visionary's. Now, in the dank darkness under the trees, with the water-filled pit nearby, the possible presence of a night prowler—any prowler—became infinitely menacing.

I spoke to Sue, for Anne still had that quality of being just beyond reach of mundane reason, though I made my voice loud enough for both girls to hear. "I think you two

148

ought to get back to town and have Anne tell the police what she saw. In the meantime, I'll look around down here—"

Anne interrupted me. "I'll do no such thing, Jason Broome. I saw what I saw and brought you both down here." It was the first time since she had surprised us on the hill that Anne had included both Sue and myself simultaneously within her remarks. Until now she had spoken to either one or the other of us, or seemed like an occult priestess addressing a larger audience.

Now her eyes passed swiftly from Sue to me and back again, and once again, more than anything else, her look reminded me of the defensive stare of some untamed creature—but there was a human quality to it now also, a desperate plea for understanding, an equally desperate intelligence.

She said, "You and Sue—I've been afraid of her from the start, Jason—from the moment she first came home. You had one thing in common I couldn't share—" her lip curled and she spoke almost with venom— "that monstrosity on the hill, your River House. You both hated it as children— Sue because it was her home and so in a sense her prison. I remember even then she liked you, Jason, and that was the reason her folks forbade you the hill. You resented it, Jason, because it was something you couldn't reach, couldn't touch—so you finally bought it, you brought the flats up there with your barroom—you made it yours, but it was hers, too—"

I heard Sue gasp beside me and sensed her small movement, though I couldn't tell whether she had pulled away from me or drawn closer. I think both our attentions were at that moment riveted on Anne—we had no accurate awareness of each other beyond what the words implied.

Anne said, "I was afraid of her, Jason, and wanted her to leave. I slashed Eloise's car and I think she guessed it—that was why she thought the vandalism was connected with—my husband's murder. When she refused to leave, I tried to destroy River House—not because I wanted you to work for my father, but because I needed someone—I needed you, Jason."

And then her wild look was gone, and love and faith were in her eyes—not quite a woman's love and faith, but those of a child.

"I needed you, Jason," she repeated almost as if by rote, and something within me responded, though it was not at all what I had felt for her before.

And suddenly I knew why she had seen something down here in the clay pit that had been invisible to both Sue and myself from up on the hill, and would have been to any other person on earth. I knew that Craddock's killer was here and she could not have mistaken him—I almost guessed his name.

Incongruously, somehow, my hand had found Sue's—or hers mine. I doubt that either of us will ever know who instigated the small movement that suddenly had us facing the world together through something that resembled a nightmare. It was not a lovers' clasp—even Anne knew that for she saw us and smiled. Then she looked away toward the tree-hidden pit as she had before, as if with vision not vouchsafed to others and said almost normally, "I want to have this over with—I want it ended—" and started to move through the trees.

Sue and I followed. I motioned her behind me and, as quietly as I could, motioned to her to go back to the car. She should have been out of this—there was no real reason for her to be here at all, beyond the reason Anne had given a moment before. A childhood crush—I remembered it now —the bitterness between us. The long nights of dreams. But none of them belonged here among grown-up realities with murder at stake.

But she followed me, and her eyes were not those of a child, but those of a woman. And the set of her face was grown-up too, with care for the moment—for me, for Anne moving ghost-like before us, and for what lay beyond.

We came to the edge of the pit, where Anne and I had stood before. The water was calm, opalescent—I could not quite see, though I could visualize, the ugly, waterlogged branches of the crabapple tree that had imprisoned the major, caught him and held him to the last.

Anne stopped there, staring at the water, and who can tell what was in her mind. Did she remember a husband, a lover, an enemy? Her face was unfathomable in the moonlight, but I remember thinking she must have ceased to love him long before he died. For love is reliance and trust and regret, and none of these were on her face as she brooded over the silent pond.

It was Sue who screamed. The sound ripped wildly through the stillness, shattering conjecture with the basic ring of truth. I remember thinking it an honest sound, a sound held in abeyance by all of us—it had that effect for me, but evidently not for Anne.

She whirled wildly and struck at Sue—in a moment the two of them were threshing on the ground. I heard Sue's gasping breath—Anne was terribly silent—and I stared at a figure across a narrow cove.

I remember only that it was a man wearing a military trenchcoat, and that he was roughly the shape and size Craddock had been. I remember the light trenchcoat, incongruous on a living man on this warm night, the oak-leaf-clusters, the MP insignia, standing out clearly in the moonlight. This I saw at a glance—simultaneously I heard a sharp, rending cry from Sue—a sound of water breaking and silence.

The figure on the other shore had vanished. Directly before my feet the water roiled. Anne and Sue had rolled off the sheer drop of the bank—with barely time for a frightened thought, I dropped in after them.

The pit here ran down steeply, but not sheerly enough for me to avoid bottom. I tasted the acrid mud, drove against it with my feet, felt the entangling branches of the crabapple tree that had cradled the major's last moments. My hand touched cloth and skin, felt two struggling forms. I wedged myself between them, breaking a death-lock by main force, using hands, fists and feet . . .

The form in my arms was limp. At the time I didn't know whether I had Sue or Anne. My lungs ached, my clothes clung leadenly—I remember a touch of panic and thinking —why hadn't I led a life that would fit me for heroics? Then my feet found bottom again and I kicked upward. I fought branches and I fought for breath. I fought a leaden weight in my arms that sought to pull me under. I fought upward and broke clear—the shore of the pit was within my reach. I grabbed vegetation and pulled and the solid bank was against my body. Sue moved feebly in my grasp. I shoved her against the embankment and gasped, "Hold on—"

Her voice was a whispered, tortured cry. "Anne—there's something—"

Behind us, in the pit, something splashed. I saw Anne's face in the moon-silvered water, her mouth opened to call out, her eyes wide and panicked. She made no sound as she vanished under the broken surface. The last thing I saw was her hand holding something—it looked like a half-brick, or dornick—and I remember wondering about it even as I got my feet against the shore of the pit and kicked.

I found them where she had gone under—two figures locked in combat. The force of my push from the shore carried me hard against them, broke them apart, and this time I had no trouble discovering Anne. Her dress was soft to my touch; her bare arm clamped around my neck. The other shape was solid, hard and moving. My hands slid over a substance that felt neither living nor dead.

But it moved as though alive. I felt the strength and resistance of it, even as Anne's arm constricted around my neck and as I thought of the weapon in her hand. A weapon against whom, or what? I felt two movements against me—hers and that of whoever or whatever was in the water with her, and in a desperate surge of self-preservation doubled my knees and kicked out.

My feet struck something solid, and we surfaced, Anne and I. Her arm was across my throat, shutting off my breath, and I brought up both hands to break that deadly hold.

Silver sprayed around us in the moonlight. Anne's face was above mine, frenetic, screaming. Her hand burst out of the water holding the dornick—she brought it against my skull with all her might.

I managed to deflect her blow partially, but the side of my head exploded nevertheless. A light bigger than the moon seemed to envelop us, and I remember struggling feebly, yet with all my might.

I remember striking her—not too hard, but hard enough to knock the half-brick out of her hand. I remember her limp and acquiescent in my arms as I struggled toward the shore. I remember her sobbing and saying my name and even helping those last few feet. . . .

And I remember those bright lights and voices, and strong hands, masculine hands, helping us both over the edge of the pit.

15

I WAS bumping belly-flat over the edge of the clay pit, and then I had my knees under me and I was getting up, and somehow I knew I was alive and would go on living. I could draw a breath and look around and ask someone what the hell?

There was no real reason why I should have been surprised to see the state police there, or Hoyle either. I had known from the start that he would be at the finish—and of course, tonight he had followed Anne. Or had her followed. And when the three of us had started for the pit, he had been notified and now he was here.

Anne stood, streaming wet and curiously listless, in a small circle of state troopers. Her eyes were empty, lifeless, until Hoyle faced her.

"It was you," she told him dully. "You spoiled everything. You went to California, damn you, and you found it all out."

I remembered that this was probably the first time she had seen Hoyle since he had returned from escorting a prisoner to the coast, remembered that he had been to the house looking for her, and that she had been running from him tonight.

Hoyle said, "I found out several things. I found you and

154

Major Craddock were married on the Coast quite some time ago."

She said, still quite lifelessly, "You still have to prove I murdered him. I didn't have a chance with you from the start, did I? But you still have to prove it."

There was something that I wanted to tell Hoyle. It was important. I tried hard to remember what it was. I was beginning to shake. I was cold to the bone. I wished I had a coat. Then I remembered—coat was the key word to the puzzle that bothered me at the moment.

I said, "Hoyle—there's someone around here tonight in an officer's trenchcoat—there's something in the water—" But Hoyle didn't hear me, or didn't want to hear me. I suppose he was a good law officer and had work to do and I was somebody who had had a bad time and he was always meeting people like that.

He said to the men who were holding Anne, "Take her away."

"You can't take me away," Anne suddenly screamed. "He was my husband. You found that out! We were secretly married in California, but you snooped around until you found out the truth. But you don't know why we kept it secret, do you? You don't know the kind of man my father is! His aide was not his idea of a marriage prospect for me. I was to marry someone important—" Her eyes reached beyond the men who were holding her and found mine. She said, "Jason, tell them—"

Hoyle barely glanced my way. He said, "We had it figured like that."

I had the shakes. I really had the shakes; and it was more than being soaked to the hide and chilled to the bone. It was all there, in one sentence, beautifully and tersely summed up. Craddock had been her husband and they had kept it a secret from her father.

I think I had known back there in the trees where Anne

had parked, who had killed Craddock. I should have known it the day she and I had parked here in the brickyard and she had told me about her father's being upset because he had found her coming fresh from the bath and fighting with Craddock. She had lied to me only a little. She hadn't told me that she and Craddock were married. But she had tried to tell me the truth about her father, and I hadn't wanted to listen. And tonight she had told me the rest—or had brought me to where I could find out the truth.

Perhaps she had hoped I might be killed. Perhaps she had even set it up with her father—I like to think that she had meant it to be a fair fight between us—the general and me—with both of us forewarned. But the general had fancied up matters by pretending to be Craddock's ghost, and Sue's scream had precipitated things.

I don't like to think that she really meant to brain me with that half-brick—or that she had known in advance that under the trenchcoat the general had worn a frogman's getup, which would certainly have given him an advantage over me in the waters of the pit.

In these ways, I disagreed with the findings at the hearing. Of course, she had known all along that her father was a murderer—and been half mad with the knowledge.

"Hoyle," a trooper called out. "There's someone moving over there—not one of our men."

I thought Hoyle didn't hear him. Hoyle had moved closer to Anne, who stood dispiritedly now, supported by two troopers.

"We never found a real motive for you, Miss Cramer," he said to her. "Consequently you were never seriously a suspect. We began to wonder a little, though, when you gave Broome his alibi." He whirled suddenly to me. "Broome, did you ever figure out why we didn't pick up your black-jack?"

"I remember bringing the matter up with you," I said

wearily. "When you didn't follow up on it, I assumed you already had the murder weapon."

"We did," Hoyle said. "It was a round stone, powdered with dirt and with some of the major's blood on it, and smooth enough for us to pick up some imperfect prints. Not enough to get a conviction on, but enough to indicate a direction. Your prints checked clear—so did most of our other suspects'. We got the general's prints from Washington, and he didn't quite clear. And he was too big a man for us to tackle without a complete case—he could have hamstrung our investigation from hell to breakfast. I think we've got him now."

They didn't though, not quite. All around us troopers' flashlights dotted the night, and presently Hoyle moved out among them, presumably to direct the search. Presently a trooper put a blanket around Anne, and another came to me and offered me one. I didn't see Sue anywhere.

The trooper said, "We've got her in a prowler. We're about ready to take her home. She was asking about you, just now, according to Hoyle you're in the clear, and if you'd like us to drop you off at River House—"

I shook my head. I wanted to see it through now. I wanted to see the thing I had fought in the water brought face to face with me, and so lay the ghost of Major Craddock forever.

The trooper saluted and left. I stood, not shivering now, and watched the lights move through the trees, and now and then I glanced at Anne. She didn't look at me once, or seem to know that I was there—she stood in total apathy. I wondered just how bad her mental crackup was, and thought of the hell she must have lived in with a father like that—what hell must have been in her thoughts when she had brought me here tonight, knowing her father was waiting, knowing she must make a choice between us.

For I have never doubted that in her way she had loved

157

me once as much as it had been possible for her to love—though she loved nothing now.

Not even life.

There was a sudden sound of a shot, and a flurry of movement among the trees, the lights converging swiftly. The one shot was echoed by others, a brief, sharp fusillade —I threw a swift glance at Anne, who appeared not to have noticed; then I ran toward the sounds.

Hoyle met me halfway—he put out his hand to hold me back. "It's all over, Broome," he said tiredly. "The general chose it this way—and we had to take him. I doubt he knew how many hit him at the end. There'll be no trial—there's suddenly no case—but we'll want you for the hearing."

"What about Anne—Miss Cramer?" I asked.

Hoyle sighed. "I doubt she'll help much. One thing I didn't tell you we found out in California. She'd been committed there once for a considerable length of time. A tendency to paranoia—they thought there that she would crack one day for good." He looked directly at me and I knew he meant it when he said, "I'm sorry as a man can be, Broome."

So was I. There didn't seem to be anything else to say. I was cold again, even under the blanket. I stood there and shivered and looked past where Anne still stood, and suddenly I couldn't bear to look at her.

Beyond her stood a prowl car, and beside it stood the trooper who had brought me the blanket and given me Sue's message. He saw me and beckoned. Evidently Sue had not left. Evidently she was waiting.

I started walking slowly toward the sleek, gray prowler.

THE END